BOURNE EVIL

•

A crime thriller
set in the
streets of Bournemouth

•

Sally Ash

First published in 2005 by
S. J. Bowers
Dorset

Copyright © 2005 Sally Ash
Cover photography by Kathryn Wentworth

ISBN 0-9550533-0-7

Printed by Creeds the Printers, Broadoak, Bridport, Dorset DT6 5NL
01308 423411

Chapter One

The boy sat alone in the darkness with his back against the cold, hard tombstone, moisture from the damp grass and ivy seeping through the seat of his jeans. The air was heavy with the smell of rotting wood and leaf mould. A breeze was gathering force, swaying the branches of the trees and scrub that kept him hidden from the narrow footpath only a few metres away. The path was dotted with a few older style street lamps which cast a pale orange glow, causing shadows to flicker and dance around him. In his hands he held a wallet of brown leather, so old and worn that cracks were starting to show along the seam. A couple of ten pound notes were just peaking out of the side. He heard footsteps coming towards him and rolled over into a crouching position, peering round the corner of the tomb. A couple of teenage lads walked past, talking in earnest tones, unaware of his presence. Then a young couple appeared and stopped right under a nearby lamp for a long, slow kiss. The boy watched them closely, licking his lips in excitement. He liked watching people 'at it'. The girl was skimpily dressed and the boy was sliding his hands right up her skirt, then round to the inside of her thigh. She let him continue for a couple of seconds only, then pulled away laughing and walked on up the path leaving him to follow eagerly in her wake.

He watched them till they had disappeared from view then sat back down, shaking his head in apparent disgust. He turned his attention back to the wallet, his fingertips gently tracing the embossed circular pattern stamped into the leather, the feel of every ridge and stitch and crease familiar in his old friend, his partner in crime. You see, he reckoned that money would get them every time. You could offer them friendship, flowers, love even, but in the end it could all be thrown back in your face. But offer them free money, in secrecy and darkness, well who could refuse? All they had to do was pick it up. He hadn't met a single one yet that wasn't stupid enough. Didn't they realize that everything comes with a price?

Eventually he heard the sound he had been waiting for, a quick tap tap tap of high heels. Rolling over onto his knees again, he took a careful look round the corner of the tomb, knowing that he was practically invisible in the shadows. A solitary female stepped into the pool of light beneath one of the lamps, walking fast, her long blonde hair flying out loose behind her. She was young and beautiful, and her skirt was achingly short. His breath quickened and his heart was pounding against his ribs. He checked around to make sure they really were alone. Nothing. You could almost say she was asking for it! He chucked the precious wallet quickly and silently into her path and waited for his prey.

The car park lay across the top of the hill, a huge expanse of tarmac marked out in bold white lines. Traffic sounds from the town below filtered through the trees which grew on three sides, the fourth being the entrance slope running alongside a tall stone block wall to the far left. Beyond the wall stood a large, stately block of grey stone flats which boasted one of the finest views in all of Bournemouth. Many of the locals could remember a time when there was a good view from the car park across the roof tops of the town to the sea, but now the trees and bushes had grown up to obscure it. The old stone steps which had once zig-zagged down the hillside into town, now took you through sloping woodland to the road below. Through the treetops on the right could be seen glimpses of the tall spire of St Peter's Church, rising up gracefully from the centre of the town.

Most of the cars were clustered round the area at the top of the steps and a couple of people stood at the pay and display machine. Apart from that, the place had a feeling of space and detachment, and Edward liked it this way. Even in the summer when the crowds thronged into the seaside town, there were always spaces here, as only the hardiest of shoppers could face the climb back up to the car park with their bags of spoils. Ed sat in his convertible BMW with his doors open and his stereo playing local radio. The hot sun beat down on the shiny red paintwork of his aging but beloved car. He fancied pulling back the black canvas top but, to be honest, it was too much effort. He hadn't bought a ticket because he wasn't planning on staying so he lit a fag, leant back and enjoyed the music. They were playing a country song and Ed had a quick check round before turning up the volume, smiling to himself that it should bother him whether or not anyone could hear.

This place was a popular hang out for the local kids in their cool cars to meet and smoke and play cool music on huge stereos with woofers that pumped out enough bass to make the earth move. Despite appearances, they weren't a bad bunch when you got to know them. When Ed saw them in town, they were either charging round and round the block, engines roaring and stereos thumping, or parked up in lay-bys, smoking and shouting.

Up here it was different. This was one of their meeting places and they seemed happy enough to park up and talk to each other in something approaching the English language, and that included Ed as the 'new kid on the block'. He looked a lot younger than his 33 years, and he supposed that his car was considered fairly 'cool'. He enjoyed seeing the different cars and acknowledged the pride with which they looked after them. He soon found that he could discuss fairly knowledgably the conversions and modifications they kept making in the name of improvement. They in turn were pleased to have someone who appreciated their efforts and the younger ones often sought him out for advice or to show off their latest gizmos and, more often than not, to scrounge his fags. He was amused by the similarities to his own teenage gang of fifteen years earlier when he had been a grunting spotty youth himself, though he came from a rural area of Dorset and his gang were into bikes. He thought fondly of his bright green Kawasaki, probably still rusting away in his fathers garage.

Today however, he found himself alone. Probably just as well. Billy Ray Cyrus wouldn't do wonders for his street cred! He checked the time, then checked his hair in the mirror. Was he vain? He didn't think so, though he had to admit what he saw wasn't too bad compared to the beer monsters you could see any night in town. He would like to have been a bit taller, but a new pair of Wrangler cowboy boots added a couple of inches without making him look a prat! He wore his shiny dark brown hair a little longer than was fashionable, and his hazel eyes were clear and direct in his lightly tanned face. Ed favoured tight jeans and fitting T shirts, often with the sleeves cut out, or black canvas jeans and an open necked shirt. He couldn't help it, he was a cowboy at heart!

He had long since removed the tiny gold hoop earring as he was told by his sister that it was a bit 'dodgy', but he had kept his gold wedding band, only removing it to his right hand. He took hold of the ring between the forefinger and thumb of his left hand and toyed with the idea of removing it. Just slip it off, it would be easy, why couldn't he do it? A sharp tap on the windscreen brought him back to his senses with a jump. Willy Nelson was drawling on the radio and Ed hastily turned it down; God, the D.J. was really spoiling him tonight! The passenger door of his car opened and Daz climbed in, a daft grin across his spotty face. "Hello mate, what are you up to? Got any fags?"

Daz was a local kid who liked to hang around with the gang, although he didn't own a car. Ed recalled a time before his own first bike when he carried a crash helmet around with him, trying desperately to fit in, or just hoping for a ride. Daz had that eager puppy look. He was short, skinny, and had sticky-up hair and a chipped front tooth. Ed suspected that he had perfected the lost and pathetic look on purpose, and that there was more to Daz than meets the eye. He held down a full time job at a petrol station, and always seemed to have enough cash on him.

"Sure!" said Ed, chucking him the packet. "Nothing much. Where are you off to tonight?"

"Nowhere special. Look Ed? Would you do me a favour?"

"Depends what it is."

"I'm supposed to be meeting some guy here Thursday night, midnight. He wants me to work for him, only I don't know much about him."

"So?" said Ed.

"I was wondering if you wouldn't mind hanging about a bit, just in case like."

"Well, for one thing," said Ed, "I'm working on Thursday night, and for another, it sounds a bit odd to me! What are you getting yourself into?"

"Oh, nothing. It doesn't matter," said Daz. "It's just that he works in a hotel or something so he finishes late, that's all."

"Well, what sort of work does he want you to do?" asked Ed. Daz wasn't the brightest kid, and Ed didn't want to see him being taken advantage of.

"I'm not sure. This bloke comes into the petrol station fairly regular for his fags, and we got chatting. He says he's offering serious money for the right bloke, and said he'll give me a try. It's got to be worth a listen."

"Fair enough. OK, but I don't want to get involved, right?"

"Thought you said you were working!"

"I expect I can get off in time."

"What do you do?" asked Daz curiously.

"Oh, this and that, you know."

Just then, a yellow Sierra with black striped paintwork came roaring up the slope blasting out bass and fumes. It was Brad, the first of the evening's arrivals. Quick as a flash Daz got out of Ed's car, then stuck his head back in.

"You'll look out for me then?"

"Yeah, course!"

"Cheers Ed. You're a mate. Don't forget will you? Got another fag?"

Ed only had three left. He took the packet back and chucked one to Daz.

"Ill be here. Don't mess me about."

Daz was already opening Brad's passenger door as the Sierra pulled up next to Ed's BMW. Ed checked his watch. He didn't want to be late for work. He pulled his door shut and started the engine. Brad shouted out a greeting and asked Ed where he was going.

"Work!" he replied.

"He won't tell you what he does," grinned Daz.

"I could do but then I might have to kill you after," shouted Ed, driving off with a wave. He knew he sounded daft but Ed had something to hide. One day they would find out, but till then….

For some reason that he couldn't fathom, his conversation with Daz had left him uneasy. If only Ed could have seen into the future then wild horses wouldn't have dragged him to the car park on that Thursday night.

Ed lived in a bedsit about a mile away near a suburb called Charminster. "Studio flat in desirable location," the card in the newsagents window had said. What caught his eye about the advert was the possibility of a garage to go with it. These were as rare as hen's teeth in Bournemouth. The house was a huge old Victorian redbrick which had seen better days. The fancy brickwork, with it's mouldings and arches, used to be a deep red, but was now blackened with years of grime. The huge windows were still wooden, some with their original stained glass, and the sills and lintels were picked out in aged yellow brick. Ed liked the house as soon as he saw it. There were similar ones all over Bournemouth, and this one reminded him of his Gran's house. She had been a remarkable woman who lost her husband in the war, and went on to run a guest house single handed on Bournemouth cliff where Ed and Lara often went to stay in the school holidays. Most of them were now split into flats or bedsits, or run as seaside B&B's. He let himself in the huge front door with the thick green gloss paint and sagging stained glass, and picked up the free papers off the terracotta tiles. The entrance hall was bare except for an old hall stand with an ancient mirror. The walls were dingy magnolia and the doors were painted white. Mr. Fellows, the owner, lived in the largest flat on the ground floor. Ed had never seen inside as Mr. Fellows liked to keep himself to himself. Every Friday morning the nine residents, most of whom were elderly, were asked to slide their rent books under his door and Mr Fellows would take the money, sign the book, and return them in a similar fashion.

Ed put the papers on the hall stand, and climbed the once magnificent staircase. The light switch was on a timer, and lit up a bare bulb on a wire. There was still a huge, dusty chandelier hanging in the stairwell, who's sparkling days were sadly over. A threadbare red and gold carpet clung to the treads, most of its pattern long gone, and the air had a slightly musty, mothball smell. Ed put his key in the white door with the brass 5 on it, and closed it behind him. This was home. The room was approximately a 15ft cube, painted a bright daffodil yellow, with a large window on the far wall. He had a modern telly and stereo, and a cooker and water heater from the ark! The fireplace was tiled in deep green fire-glazed tiles, and was probably considered bad taste, but again it reminded him of his Gran, and felt comfortable and familiar. Pity about the electric fire plonked in front of it. Still, one had to keep warm.

Ed put the kettle on and dropped some bread into the toaster. It made a change not to have to scrape the green bits off first. He took his snack to the sofa, picked up the remote and switched on the tuner. Dire Straits were playing 'Private Investigations'. The mellow guitar and laid- back voice suited his mood. He leant back and stared unfocused at the large paper globe he had bought for £4.99 from Woolworths to cover the light bulb. Though a far cry from what he was used to, the bedsit suited him fine for now. He was beginning to feel at peace for the first time since 'it' happened. He was still unable to examine the memories of the past few months, of Lisa. The hurt and the shock were still to painful to touch, so he kept them filed away to explore at a later date. However, there were times over the last few weeks when he had managed not to think of her for whole hours at a time.

It wasn't easy building a new life from scratch, completely discarding the old one. For the first time in years, his life had no direction beyond finding sanctuary, no goal other than basic survival. He would have to come to terms with the wreckage that was now his life before he could move on and make plans for the future. He didn't think he was doing too badly, all things considered. He had a home and a job of sorts, though he hadn't had time to make many real friends yet. His sister had married a French architect and they lived abroad so they rarely got in touch. He had barely spoken to his parents since the day he left. He still felt that the ultimate betrayal, the final blow, had been dealt by them, and just at a time when he needed them most. So......., he had filed his mother and father carefully away with Lisa, before cutting all ties and fleeing the nest.

Ed's family lived in the pretty Dorset village of Gifford St. Margaret, where the pace of life was as gentle as the landscape. It had one village shop, a chapel, and a small village hall for jumble sales and keep-fit classes. The local pub, The Griffin, had closed for good about eight years ago, taking with it the heart of the community for many of the residents. Once a rural farming area, it was now home to the wealthy retired, and a few hard-working couples who needed a country retreat. Ed's parents were of the former set since Ed and his sister, Lara, had left home. There were still a few farm cottages housing retired labourers but these were becoming extinct, their families selling up and moving on.

Ed had married Lisa when he was 23 and she was 21. They'd bought a small cottage with help from their parents, and they both worked in the nearby town of Wimborne Minster, her as an estate agent and Edward in engineering. Lisa hadn't wanted to start a family, preferring to concentrate on her career first. Ed simply hadn't felt ready for kids, and life was fine as things were. Nothing much changed for several years. Lisa got the longed for promotion when she was 25, and was moved to the Southbourne office, just outside Bournemouth. Her salary increase meant she could afford a better car, and Edward cheerfully took over the old Audi. He worked his way onto the design team at work, and they could soon afford to start going out more, and to have better holidays. The value of their cottage had soared, and they were really on their way up. Lisa was away most days from 7.30am to 7.30pm, and sometimes later if she had a meeting with clients. Edward never complained, in fact he was proud of his clever wife.

He couldn't really put his finger on when the change had started. She hardly seemed to be around these days and when she was she was tired and bad tempered. He put it down to the stress of her job and although it annoyed him he let her have her own way most of the time, hoping it would pass. Sometimes she really started nagging, and he started to feel less and less supportive, until suddenly they were spending whole evenings barely communicating.

Then Lisa surprised Edward with a weekend in London for his 30th birthday, and for a few days they behaved like kids again, young and stupid and in love. Things at home improved for a while too, and they both made the effort to go out more and do stuff together, but gradually they slipped back to their old ways.

Edward had long since accepted that she was the ambitious one, always moving forwards while he was standing still, and now he realised that he was getting left behind. Then, two days before his 33rd birthday, the bubble finally burst.

He came home from work at half past five to find Lisa already there. She made him a cup of tea and sat opposite him at the kitchen table. He knew instinctively that something was very wrong. Calmly, as though she had rehearsed it, she told him that she didn't want to be with him any more, that they had drifted apart too far, and that it was only fair to him to be honest while they were both young enough to start again. Edward's world seemed to disappear around him as he sat and stared at her with his mouth open. He shook his head, the words just not forming. Illogically his mind was thinking, "Rewind! Everything was alright ten minutes ago. Yes, rewind," like this was a bad video.

"What did I do wrong?" was all he could finally manage.

"Nothing," she replied. "I've tried to explain. Didn't you hear me? Anyway, its too late, I've already made up my mind." He never really knew where his next question came from, or why. It just came.

"Is there someone else?" (Light blue touchpaper and stand clear)! She was silent for a couple of seconds, and then she exploded.

"Yes there bloody well is you halfwit! Not that you'd notice, so wrapped up in yourself all the time. Anyway, he's not the reason, you are! You have no bloody idea what it takes to make a marriage work! You just think that we can drift along, not a care in the bloody world! You know nothing about me, nothing about my hopes and dreams. Have you ever had an original idea in your whole life? What have you ever achieved? You just plod on with your bloody eyes shut! You've driven me to this! Its your own fault! You're just ignorant and selfish and stupid!" Her voice had risen to screeching pitch, and as she continued her tirade he noticed for the first time fine lines around her eyes, and angry creases between her brows. Her soft brown eyes were suddenly hard, her lips had set into a dissatisfied pout. He looked at the creature opposite him and barely recognised her. When had all this happened? Whatever could have gone wrong? She continued her assault, near screaming point as guilt made her desperate to provoke some sort of response. His Lisa had a soft voice and a sweet kind face. This wasn't her, and this wasn't happening.

Confused and disorientated, Edward stumbled from the cottage, her voice ranting after him, and kept walking till he could hear her no more. Lisa finally put her head in her arms and sobbed. She didn't know what she had expected but it wasn't silence. Guilt was coursing through her. The look in his eyes would stay with her forever, uncomprehending like an injured animal. He hadn't deserved any of that. He had been a good husband. It was her who had been dissatisfied, and eventually unfaithful. She wanted to go after him, to say she was sorry, but she knew she had gone too far.

Edward couldn't remember much of what followed. Deep in shock he stumbled to the car, and then found he'd left his keys in the kitchen. He wandered down the lane and into a field with high hedges and long damp grass. He needed to be alone, to hide where no-one would find him, and sort his head out. He entered the old hay barn and curled up behind some bales where he couldn't be seen, and stayed there till next morning……

Two days later, on his birthday, he watched her go to work, then entered the cottage for the last time. He stuffed a few things into a suitcase, grabbed his guitar and an amplifier from the dining room and packed them in the boot of the car. Next he quickly sorted out his few personal papers and his bank books into a carrier bag, dropped his door key on the kitchen table and left. Lisa could have the house. Her father was a solicitor so she'd probably end up with it anyway. He drove towards Bournemouth, where he knew he should have no trouble finding a cheap B&B. Beyond that he had no real plans. He passed a used car showroom and, completely on impulse, he pulled up outside. For the first time in days a smile crossed his lips. The salesman had seen that smile before, and practically glided across the showroom floor to greet his next victim. Ten minutes later Edward had traded in his old Audi 80 for a flame red convertible BMW. It had rather a lot of miles on the clock, but it had a full service history and a warrantee, and as Edward put his foot down it shot forward and purred in a very satisfying manner.

"You and I are going to get along very nicely," he said. "What the hell! It is my birthday!"

Edward drained the last of his coffee and checked his watch. He jumped off the sofa and opened the wardrobe, carefully selecting the hanger which held his black stretch jeans and best pale blue shirt, and got changed. Next he put on his silver collar tips and shoelace necklace, grabbed his guitar and a new cowboy hat. Edward's secret was about to come out.

Ed Curran was a country singer!

Chapter 2

Bournemouth Bay is a gentle curve of pure golden sand, seven miles long, with Hengistbury Head guarding the entrance to the tranquil harbour of Christchurch at one end, and the beautiful but expensive Sandbanks Peninsular at the other. The bay boasts two piers. Boscombe pier has fallen into a state of disrepair, and has long been the subject of passionate local debate. Thankfully the structure is still sound, surviving a constant battering from sea and storm as the controversy over its future rages on.

Approximately half way along the bay is Bournemouth pier, which is a much grander affair altogether. Built by the Victorians, it was designed for a far more sedate way of life when the British seaside holiday was in its infancy and paddle steamers from Poole and Purbeck regularly moored up alongside to collect and deliver scores of excited day trippers. Hats and parasols were the order of the day as were the Punch and Judy stands, while the more adventurous got changed in one of the dozens of bathing huts which dotted the sand before taking a dip in the sea. The old Pier Theatre has survived the years, still putting on live shows throughout the summer, and beyond it, facing out to sea, is a large family restaurant. Lower decks run both sides for the use of pleasure boats and fishermen, and the open area on the end of the pier is sometimes a children's funfair. Despite a few hotly contested modern buildings, such as the huge metal and glass 3D cinema on the pier approach, Bournemouth has managed to retain much of the charm of the old fashioned seaside holiday.

Running right through the centre of Bournemouth to the sea, along beautifully tended gardens, the Bourne Stream follows a kind of natural ravine. Ablaze with flowers by day and banks of coloured lights by night, these gardens follow the stream inland for several miles to Coy Pond, once a reputed smuggling route and now a picturesque duck pond. Tall cliffs dip down where the gardens meet the sea, and the road climbs steeply each side onto the overcliff. Rows of hotels sit on the cliff tops, a grand display of elegant Victorian and Edwardian architecture tastefully painted in white or pale shades of blue, green and cream. The hotels on the East Cliff are strung out along Overcliff Drive half way back to Boscombe, and on the West Cliff the pines and chines take over, with the hotels and guest houses covering a large area inland to meet the shopping centre. Many of the hotels have bowed to the demands of the modern tourist market, and have teamed up with the coach tour operators, who ship in coach loads of OAPs for their annual week by the sea. This is how it works. The hotel offers full board and regular entertainment, while the coach operator provides the transport, plus day trips to the New Forest and surrounding villages, all for a budget price. The package coach holiday provides the mainstay for many a local musician. The money may not be as high as for the weekend social functions in the larger hotels, but it does provide precious, regular, midweek work, and once a smaller hotel finds a couple of solo or duo acts that fit the bill, it tends to stick with them.

Ed had quickly worked his way into the local hotel scene by offering to do a couple of free gigs. Once they had heard his clean, melodic voice and seen the affect his open, friendly manner had on their guests it wasn't hard to talk his way into a few regular bookings. OK, so maybe Ed had to channel his musical tastes down to suite the age group of his audience, but they were usually a lively friendly bunch, many of whom enjoyed a good dance, and the old tunes were often easier to play and sing. In the smaller hotels Ed worked alone, perched on a stool with his guitar and wearing his cowboy hat, though this tended to come off after the first half hour. He wasn't quite sure why he wore it, except that he enjoyed the sense of a new identity that it gave him. In his hat he was "Ed Curran, rising country star", and not "Edward the dumped on!"

On Saturday nights Ed was joined by Mike, a keyboard player and vocalist. Mike was a master of technical wizardry, and could make his keyboard sound like a grand piano, or a fifteen piece band, complete with brass section and drums. They had first met when Mike placed an advert in the local paper for a lead guitarist with vocals. Ed had learned to play guitar at school, and he soon found he was able to pick out the tunes he liked without music. His teachers spotted his talent early on, but his parents never took it seriously. As if Edward could ever be a professional musician? Later on Edward spent hours playing in the cottage while Lisa worked late. He knew he was good but had never got round to doing anything about it. At the audition Mike and Ed hit it off straight away, neither musician fighting to play lead, but both enjoying working with the natural talent of the other. They had both worked solo, though in Ed's case only for a few weeks, so neither had anything to prove.

Mike was a big blonde chap in his late thirties with short, fuzzy hair and a face which rarely showed any expression. He was married to Trish, a short, fiery redhead, and they had two little girls. Mike had tried to explain to Ed what his job was but as far as Ed was concerned he was just something clever in computers. They had spent many evenings together in the spare bedroom of Mikes large family home, working out their songs while Trish kept them plied with beer or tea. After she had got the girls to bed and Mike had excused himself for five minutes to tuck them in, Trish would come and sit on the bed quietly and listen to them play for a while. Ed admired the way she offered them support and encouragement, and he respected both her comments and her criticism.

She was no beauty, and the two of them weren't outwardly affectionate, but there was a sense of teamwork, of togetherness, that he knew would never waver. He thought briefly of his Lisa. Would she have been so supportive? He doubted it. More than likely the noise would have got on her nerves. Although he hadn't known them for long, he looked on Mike and Trish as his closest friends. They knew a little of his circumstances but had never probed to know more, sensing that his pain was still fresh. Once he had briefly opened up his heart to Trish, with her sympathetic green eyes and auburn hair while Mike was putting the girls to bed. They had dropped the subject on Mike's return, and Trish didn't question him further, but it was strange to have finally shared his problems with someone else, and not at all bad.

Tonight was Saturday night and the two of them were booked to play at the Victoria Towers Hotel on the East Cliff. They were both wearing dinner suits with bow ties, one of the necessities of the dinner dance circuit, and were due to play from nine- thirty till one. Ed managed to squeeze his car into the last gap in the hotel car park and found that Mike was already there. They took their gear in through the fire exit and set up along the wall on the far side of the dance floor before the guests came in. Then they settled down in a corner of the hotel bar, Ed with a beer and Mike with a coffee. This was the usual agenda for a function, and they often had to wait an hour or more before they could start, chatting about anything that came to mind. Mike started by complaining about the price of the kid's school trips and the cost of their uniforms. They then covered the subjects of football, petrol and oil prices, and had just launched into the minefield of Trish's newly planned kitchen when the duty manager asked them to start playing.

The function room was full of round tables draped with dark blue cloths, surrounded by people in full evening dress just tucking into dessert. Each table had a bunch of blue and silver balloons rising from a floral arrangement in the centre, the whole affect being one of taste and decorum. The first hour was to be a dinner set which meant 'easy listening' music played at a volume that still allowed the guests to chat if they wanted. As the desserts were cleared away and coffees started coming out, Mike selected a gentle waltz and Ed started singing Moon River. When it ended Mike continued the rhythm and sang True Love while Ed strummed gently on his guitar and sang in harmony. One couple made their way onto the dance floor, followed by a gentle ripple of applause, the man looking a little self conscious. They were joined by two more couples during the song, but they all sat down again when their coffees arrived. No-one else danced during the first set but it was still a good omen for later on.

After forty five minutes the party had to make speeches and toasts so the duo returned to the bar. Ed looked longingly at the beer pumps but ordered a coke. Mike ordered the same and the barman sent them away with a nod when they tried to pay. That was a result! Sometimes they got lucky and sometimes they didn't, but hotel prices weren't cheap and it was worth remembering a barman's face for next time! The speeches dragged on for ages, interspersed with ripples of laughter and bursts of applause. What on earth did they find to talk about? Mike and Ed knew that when they were over there would be a surge of people into the bar area, desperate for a fag. That was their cue to return to the stage.

The second set was a little louder and more for dancing. Ed and Mike had to throw in some rock and roll, disco, and Ed's beloved country music to see what got them moving. The country scored the first hit, with several couples doing a quickstep. Then they moved easily into a jive, and by the end of the second set, half the room were on the dance floor, bouncing around to anything that the duo threw at them. By this point they had taken off their black jackets and looked very handsome in their white shirts, well cut black trousers and bow ties. Some of the women had been making the most of the hospitality, (free wine), and were making eyes at them. This was a fairly usual turn of events but sadly it never seemed to be the really pretty ones!

By the end of the last set just about everyone in the room had let their hair down, and were romping away to the likes of the Rolling Stones and Status Quo. It never failed to amuse Ed to see the gentlemen, so dignified on arrival, flinging their arms and legs around with total abandon, while the ladies in their ball gowns hitched their skirts up round their knees and were stomping around to Tina Turner songs. Then, as they struck up the Last Waltz, decorum returned to the room in an instant. Circling couples reminiscent of Fred and Ginger whirled round the dance floor until the final chords of the song. At the end somebody borrowed the mic and made an announcement.

"Let's have a huge round of applause for the band! Thanks lads, you've done a great job." The room erupted and the guys grinned shyly. Ed never knew what to say at this point so he just followed Mike's lead and gave a little bow.

The barman had laid on coffee for them in the lounge to allow the room to clear a little before they packed up the gear. This was living. In some of the smaller venues you were lucky to find a barman at all at this time of night! Ed sat back and relaxed, basking in the warm glow of appreciation. He wondered what Lisa would say if she could see him now. It all seemed a world away now, and just for a second wondered if he was better off. He had never had such a sense of achievement in his whole life. He would never have known the thrill of a live performance, of having over a hundred people smiling at him, clapping him, thanking him, telling him what a great job he'd done. He felt honoured and humbled, and felt he would cheerfully have done it for free.

When they had packed up Mike went off home in his car to Trish. The applause, which left Ed on a high, barely seemed to touch him as though this wasn't real life but just a break from it. Ed didn't want to go straight back to the bedsit on his own so he found a kebab shop and bought a medium doner with chilli relish, another new discovery, and drove up to the top car park to eat it. While he felt like company, he was aware of his attire, the suit might take some explaining, and tried not to drop chilli sauce into his lap. He listened to the smooth late night sound on the local radio for a bit, then went home to bed. He drove his car into the garage leaving his amplifier locked in the boot as usual, and took his guitar up to the bedsit. When he finally dropped off to sleep it was with a slight smile on his face for the first time in ages.

At about 2.30am, just as Ed was dropping off, eighteen year old Kelly Foster was walking through Bournemouth alone after a night out with her friends. They had gone off in a car with some boys but Kelly was tired and wanted to go home. She had promised to get a taxi but found she only had a couple of quid left, so she set off on foot. She looked longingly at the path through the gardens which would get her home in a few minutes, but it looked dark and there were deep shadows among the trees. The alternative was to walk the extra half mile round, in shoes that were killing her. There were still quite a few people around, mostly drunk and wandering home like her. She made the sensible decision and pressed on along the well lit pavement. Suddenly a chorus of shouting and swearing broke out in front of her, and she saw a gang of about twenty lads all pushing and shoving each other. Kelly looked down at her short skirt and skimpy top and didn't fancy her chances of walking through them unmolested, so she quickly turned round and headed for the top of the path through the trees. It wasn't a long path, fairly well lit, and there was only a short section which couldn't be seen from the road at either end.

She set of walking briskly with her head held high, feeling a little miffed at her friends and completely unafraid. About half way along she could see a small object on the path in front of her. As she approached she could see that it was a leather wallet, square and brown and slightly scuffed. She could see money poking out the top, and a kind of round logo embossed on the front. As she stooped to pick it up there was a sudden footfall behind her and a shadow crossed her path. Instinctively she raised one arm to protect her head and spun round to face her attacker. As she did so the man tried to force something soft over her head, but her raised arm partly fended it off. With brutal strength he grabbed her free arm, his other arm going round her neck in a kind of lock. Kelly struggled and pulled away in absolute terror, completely powerless, and heard him laugh softly to himself. But he had chosen the wrong girl, and for three reasons. One, Kelly had taken a course of self defence lessons, and two, she was stone cold sober! The deadlock gave her a moment to think, and the laugh brought her back to her senses. She felt a flash of anger and remembered what she had been shown. She knew how to break an armlock, and how to make each blow tell. Quick as a flash she twisted, not away from but towards him, momentarily loosening his grip. She ducked down with a hard elbow jab and a fierce back-fist to his face and broke free. As she ran she heard him hiss in anger and start to chase her, his footsteps and breathing close behind. But the third point in Kelly's favour was that she was the school athletics star. She had ditched her shoes and was running like a gazelle. In a few seconds she had reached the road.

Her attacker gave up the chase and returned to retrieve the wallet and the shoes, cursing and winded.

"The bitch! The bloody bitch!" he muttered. His eye felt tender where she had caught it with her fist. One shoe was lying in the path but he had to hunt around for the other one which he eventually found in some long grass behind a bench. He sat down and inspected them. They were made of cheap, multi coloured plastic with narrow ankle straps and thin spiked heels. Cheap trash! Just like her! He stuffed them inside his coat, meaning to dump them in a rubbish skip on his way home. Time to move on now. He picked up his wallet and put it carefully away in his pocket.

"Next time," he said, "I'll be ready. Next time!"

A little while later a breathless Mrs Foster burst through the entrance doors of the local police station, a bedraggled and tearful Kelly in tow.

"My daughter's been attacked!" she cried dramatically.

The desk sergeant looked up sharply and didn't see any blood, so he put on his sympathetic face and picked up his pen. A squad car was despatched immediately to the scene, and an officer ordered tea and took them into an interview room. Kelly gave him a statement, with a little too much help from her mother, but there wasn't much to go on. She wasn't injured, barely bruised, her attacker hadn't used a weapon, and she could offer no description at all except that it was a man.

Her mother and the officer both lectured her on the danger of walking in lonely places at night and she had to admit now how foolish it sounded. Then she was taken home and tucked into bed with one of her mother's sleeping pills. She fell asleep surprisingly quickly, the nightmare over for now.

It was a pity that she had forgotten to mention the wallet!

Chapter 3

Next morning Ed woke at around 8.30am, and then dozed happily till about 9am. He read his book for a while and then nodded off again till gone ten. He eventually crawled out to make some tea and then sprawled on the sofa with his mug, putting the radio on for company. It had taken a while to get used to waking up alone, and he had felt desperately lonely for the first few weeks. Sunday mornings had always been planned out for him. Either Lisa had wanted him to take her out for the day, or else she had a couple of jobs lined up for him at home, and sometimes at her parents house. Edward didn't really mind. Nine years of marriage had taught him that resistance was futile, that Sunday mornings were not his own, and one really had to go with the flow.

He didn't have a problem with his in-laws, it was just that they always gave the impression that somehow Edward was a disappointment, or that Lisa had married beneath her. It was nothing they said or did but the implication was most definitely there. It used to wind him up, but more recently it had simply amused him. If they chose to believe that their darling daughter had married the village idiot then there was precious little he could do about it!

Now, Sundays were all his and he felt quite smug. He could do what he liked, when he liked, and his head was still full of the coloured lights, the smiling faces and the sound of applause from the night before. The local radio news came on and police were appealing for witnesses to an attempted mugging in the early hours of this morning in a central Bournemouth park. The victim, a teenage girl, was shaken but unhurt. Ed wondered momentarily how close he had been while eating his kebab.

He spent the day lazily, playing his guitar quietly to himself for a while, then walking into town to look round the shops, before returning home. He thought about phoning Mike and Trish, knowing they would invite him round for dinner, but settled for a takeaway pizza and some good old Sunday night telly.

On Monday Ed rose early and went for a run along the beach. The air was clear and cold, the sky a washy blue, and the tide was out leaving a golden band of firm sand at the shoreline. For the whole seven miles of beach, long, dark wooden breakwaters ran out from the promenade into the sea, splitting the sand into sections. On the end of each was a tall post where the solemn, black cormorants perched staring into the surrounding sea with concentration, looking out for breakfast. Ed liked to keep in shape and it was a few days since he had been running, so he pushed himself harder than usual, knowing he would be stuck indoors for most of the day. There was a cool light breeze which ruffled his hair as his feet pounded the promenade, and the first rays of heat from the watery sunshine landed on his face. When he finally got home, he showered and changed, and left on foot for his day job.

A short conversation with his mother on the day after he left revealed that Lisa was considering asking him for maintenance as she was worried about paying the mortgage on her own. Nice to see she'd got her priorities right! Ed had already phoned work sick, but had since written to tell them that he would not be returning. The thought of going back into an office where everyone knew his business simply did not enter his plans, but meanwhile he had to do something about money, and fast.

The day after he moved into the bedsit he had popped out to

a little grocery store in a nearby parade of shops and bought a pint of milk and some bits of shopping. In the window was a card saying, "Staff wanted, apply within." An unhappy looking Asian man sat at the till, and Ed asked him about the job. The man said that he would have to get his wife and briefly disappeared. He returned with a large lady with enormous earrings and huge brown eyes like a cow. She looked Edward up and down and gave him an indecently flirty smile.

"Oh you will do me very very nicely" she said before Edward had even spoken. He was quite taken aback. He asked about the duties and told her he had no experience of shop work.

" That's all right, I can see you are a bright boy and I will train you myself. Personally!"

Her husband shook his bald head and muttered something into his newspaper. The job was for three days a week, sometimes four or five, and the pay was appalling. Fine. Let Lisa get maintenance out of him now! The store was open seven days a week, eight till late, and they wanted to have someone in regularly so that they could have a break. The arrangement worked out well and the job was not unpleasant. They found Ed to be polite, reliable and flexible, and treated him these days more as a friend. This morning Pearl (that was not her real name but she had read it in a book and thought it sounded romantic), was waiting for him with tea and toast, and enjoyed fussing round him like a mother hen. Like Trish she had learned a little of his story but unlike Trish had demanded all the details, and seemed to have made it her mission to make him feel loved and wanted in a way that his own family never had.

Mr Patel was a daytime telly addict, and looked very sad when he was called away to work the till. He was a quiet and undoubtedly a long suffering kind of man, always polite but always worrying about something. The little deli counter was definitely his domain and his pride and joy. He carefully checked it and cleaned it each morning, and although Ed served from it, Mr Patel liked to get to the deli counter customers first. Mrs

Patel, or Pearl, was a very strange character, one day all bossy and motherly with Ed, and the next day flirting with him outrageously. She wore bright colours and large flowery patterns, and lots of jewellery with bright coloured beads and stones. She had a fierce, quick temper, and although she had never lost it with Ed (yet), she was often seen brandishing a jar or tin at her husband in a very menacing fashion, and boy could she shout!

Ed was fascinated by her eyes. They were huge and deep brown, the most gorgeous eyes he had ever seen, and there was no doubt that she had been a most attractive woman in her time, probably still was if you liked that sort of thing. Edward flirted right back and the two of them often ended up giggling while poor Mr. Patel hid out the back with his telly. Ed had once asked him how they met.

"I swapped her for a cow." He replied. "It was a fair deal, she was a poor milker!"

The next few days were spent either working or hanging around town. He had written a few songs alone in the bedsit with his guitar, but wasn't brave enough to play them to anyone else yet. They contained a lot of his most private feelings, and to play them to another soul would be like laying his heart open for inspection. Maybe one day there would be someone special enough, but for now, his trust in human nature had worn a little thin. Ed also enjoyed wandering round the shops and department stores, and loved having new clothes, though his budget was a bit limited at the moment so he had to content himself with window shopping. He had never minded taking Lisa shopping in Bournemouth, and had encouraged her to try things on. Clothes always looked good on Lisa, she had that kind of figure. He had usually treated her to lunch at Beales or Dingles, and sometimes they had carried on into the evening, ending up in a club or wine bar. Those had been the good days, when they had been young and everything was an adventure. Looking back, Ed thought that he had been a pretty good husband. He was generous and attentive, and all in all Lisa had wanted for nothing. Perhaps it was his fault that she had become spoilt and selfish. He had to confess that at some point the glitter had started to fall off, but surely every married couple had to settle down to some kind of routine together! After all, how else were things like loyalty and trust supposed to develop? He could see now that the comfortable domesticity in which Edward had thrived had left Lisa dissatisfied and wanting more, hence her almost aggressive absorption with her career. His friend Anne had once hinted that whatever Lisa was doing, she would always want more, and Ed had to reflect sadly that maybe it was true, and that no man could keep her happy for long. Lisa's love came with a 'sell-by' date, and that had included her love for him!

On Thursday night he was due to play solo at the Oaklodge Hotel from eight-thirty till eleven. He got ready, grabbed his hat and guitar and left in plenty of time. The Oaklodge was a regular booking and he was on friendly terms with the owner, who had sold up his bar in Spain to return to his home town of Bournemouth about five years ago. He nodded a greeting to Tony the barman, then set up his gear on the stage which was actually a collection of beer crates with plyboard sheets on top, the whole thing then covered with an old blue carpet. At the back of the stage, hanging floor to ceiling, were some glittery gold drapes, probably a relic from the seventies. A matching gold frill had been tacked along the front edge of the stage. In comparison the small square parque dance floor was freshly polished and in good condition. Tonight the coach party were from Wales, and were a lively noisy bunch. Although quite elderly, this party wanted to line dance so Ed had plenty of opportunity to play his beloved country and western music like the 'Mavericks' and 'Achey Breaky Heart' followed by a slosh or two. It was when they requested 'Agadoo' that he realized his street cred was going straight out the window, but he gamely went along with it seeing how they were having such a good time. The elderly folk of

Gifford St. Margaret never behaved in this manner, and it still amused him to watch, especially when he played 'Crazy', and a few started smooching like teenagers at the village disco. Some of this lot were eighty if they were a day!

After the gig the barman offered him a drink so Ed requested half a lager and sat down for a moment. The owner joined them and started to entertain them with his stories of his life in Spain and soon they were roaring with laughter. Suddenly Ed remembered his midnight appointment with Daz, slung his gear in the car and shouted his goodbyes. He left the hotel at five to twelve. When he arrived it was six minutes past and there was no sign of Daz. It was a still night and the car park was dark and deserted. Either no-one had turned up or else he had missed the action. Unsure what to do next, he got out of the car and wandered round, lighting a fag. All was quiet and most of the cars were parked on the far side, near the top of the steps. The only car at this end was a large white saloon with tinted windows. Ed assumed it was empty but as he passed, the engine started and the car pulled away, probably a courting couple up to no good. He didn't pay much attention but noticed the oval Ford badge on the rear as it swung away from him.

A couple of minutes passed and Ed was thinking about leaving when a sudden shout came from the trees on his left. He ran across but came to a fence. He wasn't quite sure what he'd heard but there was a lot of noise coming from the nearby clubs and it was hard to distinguish individual sounds. The shout came again, a young mans voice, clearer this time and it sounded a bit like he was calling 'Ed'! There was a metal rail across the exit at the back of the car park and Ed ran through the gap in the trees just beyond it, his heart thumping. It was probably only kids. He found himself facing a block of flats at a dead end in the road. On his left stood an ancient looking pair of gateposts, about 4ft apart and carved from some sort of yellow stone, much corroded. Beyond the posts lay a path, winding steeply down into the woods. Ed had never used this route before and was unsure where it lead. The orange lamps cast a dim peach glow with deep shadows, and Ed paused. "Daz!" he called into the gloom, "Daz!" There was no response so he set off down the narrow winding path looking nervously around him. There was something pale in the trees on his left. My God it was a tombstone, small and in the shape of a cross, half covered in ivy and moss. A little further down there were more, half buried in the undergrowth, some broken and some plain slabs with worn lettering. The wind rustled in the leaves and the whole thing gave Ed the creeps. It was like a bad stage set from an old horror movie.

Suddenly there was a panicked shout, nearer this time.

"No! Get off! No!"

"Daz!" yelled Ed and broke into a run, twisted trees and eerie graves flashing past him. He came to a huge rectangular tomb in the middle of the path, and just past it the path widened out into a large cemetery which sloped down to the side wall of St. Peters Church. He heard running footsteps and a door slam, and was just in time to see a large white car pull away from the lych gate and screech round the corner. Confused he ran down to the road and then looked back towards the massive stone base of the church. Facing him, against the side wall, was a long wooden bench where half a dozen lads were horsing about and completely ignoring him.

"Cut it out!" yelled one. His mates started jeering him. The lad ran at them, fists flying.

"I said get off me," shouted another. They all joined in pushing and shoving and Ed smiled to himself feeling foolish, finally seeing the reality of what he'd heard. God that weird path must have really spooked him! He continued out of the lych gate and turned left up the road to the bottom of the stone steps. He climbed back up to the car park muttering "Bloody Daz," under his breath. Then he drove straight home and poured himself a large beer to calm down.

Ed lay awake in bed for ages. Sleep just wouldn't come. He kept hearing shouts in his head, and someone calling his name. What if it had been his name? Why hadn't Daz shown up? Perhaps Daz had asked for his help because he had been afraid of someone. Perhaps Daz had been there and it had gone wrong and Ed had been too late to help him. Daz had trusted him and he hadn't been there. Ed wished he hadn't been late. Then he would know whether Daz had shown up or not. Had he been snatched? No of course not! What was that white car doing there? Those bloody gravestones! Why on earth had they been neglected like that? No wonder he couldn't bloody sleep.

He gave up and got out of bed. He strummed gently on his guitar till the lady downstairs banged on her ceiling with a broom. More guilt! Ed went back to bed, and this time he fell asleep.

Next morning he woke late and skipped his run. He felt exhausted from a bad nights sleep and went to work feeling jaded. Pearl was waiting for him in a bright pink mu-mu with huge turquoise tiger lilies on it and gold sandals with tiny bells on.

"Good morning Ed. Oh my goodness look at you!" she cried, as she jingled across the floor towards him. "What is wrong with you? I tell you, you are not eating properly. You are peaky!"

"I'm OK Mrs P, really! Late night, that's all."

"That doesn't mean you are eating properly. I will get you something. And you call me Pearl!" she purred. An angry voice came from the stockroom.

"That is not your name. It is foolish nonsense. Use the name you were given!"

"I didn't choose my name, my mother did and look at her taste. She liked you!" Ed had to smile as he went into the stockroom for a duster and some polish. Mr. Patel was glaring balefully from the corner. If Ed hadn't known better he would have said he was scared to come out.

" I live with a mad woman!" he muttered.

"Quite possible!" replied Ed, "But at least your life is never dull," and went off to polish the counters. Pearl was jangling around in the back and emerged with a mug of scalding coffee and a large iced doughnut. She hovered nearby to make sure he ate it, and although it looked a bit sickly, he had to admit that he felt better after. So much for a healthy diet! Mr. Patel was going to the cash and carry and, thankfully, Pearl had decided to go shopping today so he could look forward to a little peace and quiet. Mrs. Patel was probably the first person he had ever met who could actually kill you with kindness!

When they had both gone Ed swept up then re-stocked the tins. He then sat at the counter and wished he didn't have to work today. If only he could go and find Daz he would feel better. He decided to drive straight over to the petrol station after work and see if Daz was working. He thought of what he'd like to do to Daz when he got his hands on him. That was the last time he'd do anything like this for a mate. Especially a dozy little runt like Daz!

Mr Patel returned with some boxes and Ed carried them from his van into the stockroom for him. When he had finished he could hear a re-run of the Sweeney just starting on cable TV. Perfect timing! When it was time for Ed to leave, Pearl still hadn't returned and Mr. Patel was looking nervous.

"Are you worried about your wife, Mr Patel?" he asked.

"No Edward, but she has my credit cards. It is these that I am worrying about!"

Ed made a speedy getaway and immediately fetched his car out of the garage. He drove straight over to the petrol station where Daz worked, a couple of miles away and filled up while he was there. There was a middle aged woman on the till and he asked her when Daz was working. She said that Daz was supposed to have been in at midday but hadn't turned up. It was the first time he hadn't rung in either and the boss wasn't happy, so she would have to work the night shift as well. Ed thanked her and drove off with nagging doubts forming at the back of his mind. He wondered how to find out where Daz lived. He was sure someone would know. Daz had told him a while back that he lived with his mother somewhere near Kinson. He also told him about his Dad, who he had clearly worshipped, and who had died of cancer a couple of years ago. Apparently, his Mum had got a new boyfriend called Les, and they didn't want Daz around. She had also started using drugs, and she enjoyed her drink so she didn't seem to notice when he stayed out most nights, often sleeping rough under the pier.

Ed's heart went out to Daz, who seemed so young and completely harmless. No wonder he hung around looking for company so much of the time. He drove up to the car park to see if any of the gang were around but it was too early. He was hoping to find Brad because he knew he let Daz ride with him sometimes when he hadn't got a girl in tow. Ed pulled back the roof of his car and put the radio on, settling down to wait. He must have dozed off because next thing he knew it was dusk and the car park inspector's van was pulling up near him. Ed shook the sleep off quickly and started the car. He drove into town and picked up a burger and fries from MacDonalds and drove back up to the car park to eat it, melting cheese and sauce dribbling on his lips. Mmmm, lovely! There were a couple of kids in hot-hatches parked up at the back and eventually Brads yellow and black Sierra roared up the slope to join them. Ed wandered over to his open window and offered him a cigarette. Brad smiled up at him.

"I promised my mum I'd give these up," he said, taking one.

"Sorry Mum," replied Ed. "How can I find Daz?" Brad replied that he didn't know where Daz lived but from what he'd heard he lived with his mum somewhere near Kinson.

"Why d'ya want him?"

"Oh, we were supposed to meet up yesterday but he didn't show. He didn't turn up at work either."

"So the guy's a total waste of space. I'd let him get on with it."

"I've just got this bad feeling about some people he's seeing at the moment. He's such a dope and I'd hate to see him being used."

"Well if you're that worried, I know Simon took him home a few weeks back, soft git!" said Brad. "Mind you, it wasn't half raining hard."

"Do I know Simon?" asked Ed.

"Yeah. Simon! Drives that white Golf. Usually up on the cliff. He's only a kid, bit posh though. Mummy bought him the car for his eighteenth. Paid for the insurance too, lucky bugger!"

Ed laughed. "I know him. I bet they're all up there tonight, being Friday."

"Spect you're right. You going up there? I'll probably be along later."

"Yeah, might as well. See ya! "

"See ya!" Ed went back to his car and drove off, beeping his horn as he went down the slope. He didn't know why he did that, only that they all seemed to do it.

On the East Cliff, half way to Boscombe, there was a big lay-by marked out into parking bays facing out to sea with the pavement running in front. Beyond the wire netting fence there were a few feet of wiry grass and then the cliff fell away steeply to the promenade below. It was getting dark and lights could be seen twinkling far away across the sea on Purbeck. A few boats were still pottering about below, most with their red and green, port and starboard lights showing. Ed could just make out the distant shape of a dark tanker right on the horizon. There was a hint of orange left in the sky, the remainder of a golden sunset.

Most of the people parked nearby hadn't come to admire the view. That was left to the last few holidaymakers who had wandered out for a breath of fresh air after their dinners in the large hotels over the road. They looked warily at the lads with their flashy cars as they wandered past, who were just standing around smoking and doing nothing much as usual.

Ed saw the white Golf and walked up to the guy leaning against the side.

"Are you Simon?" he asked.

"No! That's him." He replied, pointing to a kid who looked about fifteen with several girls hanging round him.

"Thanks!" As Ed approached he could see that Simon was a handsome little sod, and he was wearing some really nice gear. "You Simon?"

"Who wants to know?"

"Are you?" tried Ed again.

"Hang on girls." He said as he walked over. Ed wondered when was the last time he'd had to say "hang on girls," if ever?

"Hiya!" grinned Simon,

"Hi, Ed!" said Ed.

" I know you. Red BM."

"Guilty!" said Ed. God this was hard work. Why were men so useless at this sort of thing. He tried again. "Some of the guys thought you might know where Daz lives."

"Why? He owe you money?"

"Something like that," replied Ed. To his surprise Simon came straight out with the goods.

"I don't know his address but I could show you if you like. You around tomorrow?"

"I can be," said Ed. "What time?"

"Meet me here at eleven. Mum wants me home for lunch by one." Ed couldn't help liking Simon despite himself.

"Thanks mate, that'll be great. See you tomorrow then."

"Yep, see you!"

And with that sorted, Ed went off home.

Chapter 4

On Saturday morning Ed drove into the lay-by on the cliff top to find that Simon was already waiting for him. He had parked broadside across two spaces and was leaning on the fence looking out to sea, his dark shiny hair blowing in the wind. He turned when Ed pulled up and waved a greeting, a broad grin on his handsome young face. He was slim and approximately Ed's height. Another couple of inches taller and he could have been a male model. He was wearing baggy jeans, a plain white T-shirt and red and white trainers. Despite the casual look Ed could tell that it was all expensive gear and Simon wore it well. He sauntered over to Ed, hands thrust deep in his jeans pockets.

"Your car or mine?" he said.

"Take mine! Save your petrol."

"OK. I'll just straighten up." Simon hopped back into his car and parked straight, then locked up. He climbed in next to Ed and they set off with Simon giving directions. He was very well spoken and Ed was impressed that he didn't try to disguise the fact.

"Thanks for doing this," said Ed. "Its really nice of you".

"No problem! I would only have been working for my Dad this morning. Either that or my Mum would have made me study." Simon told him that he was studying law at Southampton University, and his family were clearly very proud of him. His Dad ran a successful plumbing business, which came as a surprise to Ed, and his two older sisters were both something big in P.R. It sounded as though Simon was spoiled rotten, but he was still a nice kid. Ed reflected that some people were simply born with it all.

They passed through the outskirts of Bournemouth towards Kinson and drove into a large housing estate, probably built during the sixties and seventies. Simon was less sure of his directions now and they had to double back several times. Most of these roads looked the same and Ed was growing sceptical.

"Down there!" said Simon for the tenth time. Ed turned right and Simon visibly brightened.

"That's it!" he said, pointing and looking pleased with himself.

"Are you sure?" Ed asked doubtfully.

"Yep! I remember," said Simon with conviction. They pulled up outside a neat little red brick semi with a tidy little front garden. There were brightly coloured curtains hanging in the windows and cheerful flowers planted along the path which lead to a freshly painted red front door. Ed hadn't imagined Daz's mother living in a house like this.

Simon said he'd wait in the car so Ed walked up the path and knocked on the door. It was answered by a woman not much older than himself. She had short, spiky, bleach blonde hair and clear blue eyes. She was dressed in blue pedal pushers and a pink T shirt and was fairly short with a neat but curvy figure. Ed was sure he must have the wrong house.

"I'm sorry to bother you but does Daz live here?"

"Not so you'd notice," she replied, a wry smile on her pink lips. "What do you want him for?"

"He was supposed to meet me last night and he didn't show up. I wanted to make sure he was OK."

"I haven't seen him, I'm afraid. Are you a friend of his?" Ed nodded thoughtfully.

"I suppose so."

"You'd better come in then."

"I can't really, thanks. My friend's waiting in the car."

"Oh! Look, I'm sorry if I'm not being much help but Daz does what he wants to do. I haven't set eyes on him since Tuesday or Wednesday but I'm sure he's OK. What's your name? I'll tell him you called."

"I'm Ed. And you?"

"Sharon." She replied. Then she looked at him, her blue eyes suddenly sad. "If you see him…"

"I'll smack his bum and send him home!" he finished. She laughed.

"I'd be grateful," she said. "I really do worry about him but you know what he's like. I wish all his friends were as nice as you."

"Look," said Ed on impulse. "If I give you my mobile number, will you let me know when he shows?"

"Yes, OK. He's not in trouble is he?"

"Not that I know of."

"Good! It's nice to meet you Ed."

"Nice to meet you too," he said. And he meant it. On first impressions he was definitely prepared to give Sharon the benefit of the doubt, despite what he'd heard to the contrary.

Ed was quiet on the way back, deep in thought. Simon in comparison talked non-stop for a while, then asked Ed what was up.

"What do you make of Daz?" Ed needed to know.

"Don't know him really. Bit of a loser I suppose. Why?"

"Oh, a few things that don't add up."

"Can't see why your wasting your time on him."

"No! Neither can I!" laughed Ed.

"So," said Simon, "Instead of worrying about losers, show me what this old bucket can do!"

"Are you talking about my car?"

"Yep!"

"Bucket?" asked Ed in mock horror. "From someone who

drives a tarted up shopping trolley?"

"She'd beat the crap out of yours any day."

"Yeah?"

"Yeah!"

"OK, you've asked for it." Ed diverted towards the dual carriage way hoping to God that there were no police around. He rounded the roundabout and floored the gas. The BMW shot forward with little more than a purr, gathering speed at an alarming rate till she flew like a bird. The top was down and the force of the wind took Simon's breath away. Hearing his gasp, Ed stole a sideways glance and laughed. After the throaty roar of the souped-up Golf, the quiet power of the BMW was impressive. After just over half a mile, Ed eased off the speed and said,

"Well?"

"Not bad!" replied Simon. "In fact it's bloody terrific!"

"Thanks," said Ed modestly, but pleased in spite of himself. It was the first time he had really had a chance to show off in his car and looking at Simon's flushed face and sparkling eyes, it was possible that his street cred had just been raised a notch. It also occurred to him that he had gained one, possibly two, new friends today.

For the next few days Sharon's troubled blue eyes haunted him more than he cared to admit. Everyone had told him that Daz would turn up and he probably would, but he still couldn't get her sad face out of his mind, and he wished that he could do more to help her. He knew that her distress was only the natural concern of a mother for her son, and at this point he was forced to reflect bitterly on his own family. He was also painfully aware that he still hadn't given his mother his new mobile phone number, but every time he thought of talking to his parents, his mind seemed to shut down. It was most curious. He consoled himself with the thought that they had his address if they needed to get in touch with him, which seemed highly unlikely! So there he was, lying on the sofa and about to watch telly when his brain had started picking over the pieces of the puzzle once more. He forced his mind back to the task of calling his mother and found that he still couldn't face it, so perhaps now was the time to open that file and to see why it all still hurt so much. He lay there and shut his eyes, trying to remember the days before he left Gifford St Margaret.

He had spent the night in the hay barn and it was cold and miserable. He had cried and slept, and cried and slept until about eight in the morning when someone walked in and lifted the bale next to him.

"Good God!" came a woman's startled voice. Then as he turned his face towards her, "Edward, is that you?" It was Anne Crabtree, a lady in her sixties who lived in a large house and kept horses. She kept herself to herself most of the time and had a deep voice and a weathered face which hadn't known make-up for at least twenty years. At the sight of Edward's tear-stained face her faded grey eyes softened and she put down the bale she was holding.

"Come along! Tea!" she commanded walking briskly off towards the house, her fingers tucking stray wisps of grey hair into her pony tail. Then she stopped and turned. "Don't worry, no-one knows you're here. And bring the bale!" Ed found himself automatically picking up the bale and following her departing back. Such was the demeanour of Anne Crabtree that when she gave an order, both horses and humans alike generally obeyed without question. They went into a large untidy kitchen and Anne filled a huge kettle and dumped it on the Aga. Then she turned to Ed and pointed to the bale.

"Put that outside!" He put the bale just outside the door, as Anne continued.

"So! She left you did she? Silly girl doesn't know when she's well off. Don't look like that! Not much goes on around here that I don't get to hear about." Ed looked at her in surprise as she rattled around the stove with a teapot and some chipped bone china mugs.

"She's still there," he said pathetically. "I don't know what to do."

"You'll drink your tea while its hot, that's what you'll do." Edward obediently sipped from the scalding mug. Anne sat down opposite and watched him with concern in her eyes. She suddenly reached her roughened hand across the pine table, covering his.

"Do you want to tell me about it?"

"Not really."

"Then I'll tell you something. I suppose this all happened yesterday? Well, it happened to me over twenty years ago, and it took me an age to get over it. Not sure if I've got there even now! I was lucky you see, I had my horses so I had to keep going. But you can take all the time you need. Meanwhile, you're welcome to my hay barn but I think you'll find one of the spare bedrooms more comfortable, and no-one will bother you. What do you say?" Edward looked up at her kind, plain face in surprise, and managed his first small smile.

"I'd say thank you," he replied.

"That's settled then. I eat breakfast at eight, lunch at one and dinner at seven. I see you have a watch so there's no need for me to call you. Just come down if you're hungry. Now I must feed those blasted horses or there'll be a right rumpus!"

So there he was in a strange bedroom with thirty year old wallpaper, a black iron bedstead and a huge window which overlooked the fields and thankfully faced away from the village. She had brought him a newspaper and a packet of custard creams. For a long time he just lay on the bed feeling numb, and thinking about nothing at all. Then he must have nodded off. When he woke up he attacked the biscuits and looked at the newspaper. He found it hard to concentrate as the words seemed to cross over on the page before his eyes and after a while he folded it and put it down. Anne hadn't been to see him and he began to wish she would. At about half past six he ventured downstairs to be met by the glorious smell of roasting.

"Hello stranger!" said Anne. "Hope you like chicken."

"Love it," replied Edward.

"Good! Knew you'd get hungry soon!" He sat and watched her preparing the vegetables and thought what a shame it was that she was alone. He was surprisingly hungry. Maybe not so surprising as he realised he hadn't eaten properly since lunchtime the day before.

After dinner Anne washed up the pots, pans and dishes at the huge white butler sink while he dried up with an old green checked tea towel, full of holes.

"Are you going back upstairs or would you like to come and watch telly with me?" she asked. "It's a long time since I had any company." They watched M*A*S*H together in companionable silence, and then the news, with Anne tutting and clicking her tongue at any item which gave her displeasure. She disappeared for a minute, then came back with two mugs of steaming cocoa. Edward couldn't remember the last time he'd had cocoa, and was surprised how good it tasted.

"I'm treating you like an invalid, aren't I ?" she said. "I hope you don't mind but I don't know quite what to do with you."

"You're just great." said Edward . "I don't know how I'll ever be able to thank you for this. I'll try and be out of your hair soon."

"Get on with you! I said you could stay as long as you like and I meant it. Truth be known, I'm quite enjoying having a man about the place for a change. I think maybe you should let your mother know where you are though. I expect she's worried."

"I will. I'll go and see her tomorrow," said Ed. "I think I'll go upstairs now. Thanks for the cocoa, and everything."

"Goodnight Edward. Oh, and take this paper with you." She handed him the Bournemouth Evening Echo.

"OK. Thanks! Goodnight Anne."

He felt surprisingly at peace as he got into bed. Anne, with her brisk no-nonsense manner and her rough and ready hospitality, was such easy company. So much easier than going back to his parents would have been, with their probing questions and their highly vocal opinions. It was weird. He knew that he should feel broken hearted, but at the moment the whole thing was like a dream, and reality was somewhere else. He knew that he was just existing for the moment, marking time, until soon he would have to wake up and face the music. But for now he just wanted to sleep.

Next morning he rose early and joined Anne for breakfast; tea and toast. She was relieved to see that he looked a little more rested, and there was some colour back in his cheeks. When she went out to the shops, he found the newspaper that she had given him the night before and started to read at the kitchen table. This time it was easier to focus and concentrate on the page in front of him. He found himself reading the accommodation pages, and a vague idea started to form in his mind. He scanned the local items and the entertainment pages. He had been a village boy all his life, but it seemed as though everything was happening in Bournemouth. Bedsits were cheap and available, and the idea of simply running away and starting afresh was suddenly very appealing. It didn't even have to be for long. The only other option was to go back to his parents house, but he really couldn't face that and he didn't want to be a burden on them either.

Anne returned from her shopping and offered him lunch. He looked at his watch and realised with amazement that it was 12.45pm.

"Now don't be cross," she said, looking straight at him. "I've just seen your mother in the village shop and I told her where you are. She wants you to go and see them this afternoon, so I said you would."

"Oh! That's fine. Thanks Anne."

"Good! Cheese on toast OK?"

So Edward found himself traipsing up his parents drive,

with the immaculate lawn and the box trees carefully trimmed into perfect little spheres. Somehow he was aware that they looked faintly ridiculous after Anne's homely chaos. Funny how he'd never even noticed those trees before. His mother came to the front door and let him into the freshly hoovered hall. His father was waiting for them in the lounge, with its deep pile carpet and plumped up cushions. He stood with his back to them, staring into the ornate gilt mirror over the fireplace, and turned to face them as Edward and his mother entered the room. Everything seemed to give the impression that it had been placed there to impress. He had the odd sensation of being a stranger, entering this house for the very first time.

"You've come then!" said his father accusingly. So much for the fatherly concern! His mother chimed in too.

"Lisa came round last night and told us all about it. She was worried about you." (OK, so maybe he should have seen that one coming)!

"Lisa? Worried?" he cried. "So she should be after what she's done!" The first notes of indignation had crept in his voice.

"She's very upset. She didn't know who else to turn to," said his father.

"You mean she wanted to get her side in first!" responded Edward.

"To her credit Lisa has been very honest with us." His father's voice had started to rise with impatience. "We are not going to take sides Edward. Your Mother and I are very fond of you both. And quite frankly my lad, this attitude is not going to help you one bit!" Edward felt his hackles rise, angry at the turn in direction the conversation had taken.

"Lisa, my wife, has found someone else! She's been having an affair for God knows how long behind my back. What the hell has she got to be upset about?"

"Edward!" exclaimed his mother. "Don't you talk to us like that! We only want to help. There are two sides to every story you know," she added knowingly.

"And just what the hell is that supposed to mean?"

"Edward!" said his father. "We are your parents. We do know what you're like."

Edward looked at them both, feeling like he'd just been stabbed in the heart. Again!

"You know nothing about me." He spoke so quietly that they could barely hear his last words. The sense of betrayal, of anger and humiliation were just too much to bare.

"I'm going to Bournemouth," he said. "I'll be in touch." And with that he turned smartly and walked out of the house for the last time.

Anne was waiting for him in the kitchen. He kept his head down as he walked past her.

"Edward?" she said.

"Sorry Anne. I'm going to my room."

"Edward!" she called sharply. He stopped half way up the stairs. "Tell me what happened?" He fell silently to his knees, unable to go on. She came up the stairs behind him and put a hand on his shoulder. She could feel him shaking as he sobbed silently.

"Oh Edward, I'm so sorry." He looked at her with big fat tears sliding down his cheeks.

"What did I do wrong? I've never been any bother to them. I never got into drink or drugs or anything. I've always paid my way. I've tried to be a good son Anne, I really have. They've listened to Lisa's side of the story, but they're not interested in hearing mine. Why do they have to take her side? Why take sides at all?" His grief and sorrow poured over her and the cruelty of it made her angry. She spoke clearly and slowly, as if to a child.

"Edward. Listen to me. I probably shouldn't tell you this, but then I never could keep my big mouth shut. I've known your mother since she was a little girl. I used to baby-sit for her mother you see, your gran. 'Stuck-up Suzy Smith' the other kids called her, and they weren't wrong. She used to put on these airs and graces, and look down her nose at the other kids. It didn't make her very popular as I recall, and it was such a relief when she met your father. Like two peas in a pod they were. Some people go through life so wrapped up in themselves that they lose touch with what's going on outside. They have a lovely home and surround themselves with nice things, but are they really happy? How many real friends do you suppose they have?" Ed was quiet for a moment while he thought about this. He couldn't remember anyone popping in for a chat, not with his Mum or his Dad, ever! So, who was all the show for exactly? Anne carried on.

"Your mother was most put-out this morning when I told her you were staying with me. That's probably why she was so hard on you. Now they really do care very deeply about you Edward, but people like your parents also care about appearances, and I dare say that a divorce in the family won't suit them at all. You might not like them very much at the moment, but do try to understand them a little. That way, at least you will see that none of this is your fault." Edward was silent whilst taking on board this new perspective.

It was hard to look objectively at your own parents, and to see them and judge them as others might. For the first time in his life he tried to step back and distance himself, to see them from a different viewpoint, and he wasn't very proud of what he saw. So, for now, he would have to shrug off their hurtful comments and misguided snobbery. All that mattered for him at present was survival. He had to be strong, not just for now but for the foreseeable future, and after all the upset and inactivity of the last few days, he found that he was almost looking forward to the challenge.

Anne lifted her hand as his sobbing subsided and turned back down the stairs.

"Anne," he called after her. "I need to talk to you about something else." She turned and looked him straight in the eye.

"Good!" she said briskly. "I see you've made a decision. I'll put the kettle on." Good old England, where a cup of tea was the standard prescription for any crisis!

Chapter 5

The ring tone of Ed's mobile phone brought him sharply back to reality and his arm reached out towards the coffee table. Then he realized that he'd left it in his jacket pocket which was hanging on the back of the door. He let it ring. His memories had left him feeling a little down and he didn't feel like talking to anyone just yet. He looked at his watch. It was nearly six. He was playing at the Hollycroft tonight, but he didn't need to leave for over an hour.

After he'd showered and changed, he picked up his mobile. The missed call was another mobile number, one that he didn't recognise. Curious now, he returned the call and it was answered by a female voice, sounding young and a little nervous. It turned out to be Sharon, wanting to know if he'd heard anything of Daz.

"Hasn't he come back yet?" asked Ed.

"No! Its been over a week now and I'm getting worried. Do you think I should go to the police?" Ed thought to himself that maybe he should have gone to the police days ago.

"Has he done this sort of thing before?"

"Yes. A couple of times. Look, I'm sorry to bother you. It's really not your problem."

"No, I want to find him too. Tell you what," said Ed. "I'm busy tonight, but tomorrow night I'll go and find his mates. I know where most of them hang out and someone must have seen him."

"Would you really? I don't suppose I could come with you could I? I need to be doing something, only I don't know where to start. I feel like I barely know him these days."

"Yes. Of course," said Ed, "I'll pick you up. It won't be till about seven though."

"Don't worry. I can get the bus."

"I said I'll pick you up. But only if you'll let me buy you a drink."

"I think I'd better buy, after all the trouble I'm putting you to."

"Well that will give us something to argue about when you get here! Seven OK?"

"Yeah, fine!"

"Good. Keep your mobile handy won't you. I don't know if I can find your house again."

"Sure. Bye then."

"Bye."

Ed put the mobile down thoughtfully. He hoped she hadn't got the wrong idea. He didn't want her to think that he was hitting on her. After all, she had only come to him for help. She really wasn't his type, and anyway, she had a boyfriend already. Daz had told him that much. He wondered idly when he would be able to start thinking about having a girlfriend again.

That evening passed pleasantly enough. Looking back, Ed thought of it as the lull before the storm. There was only a small crowd staying at the hotel, and they weren't really dancers, so Ed kept them happy by taking requests. He found that he knew a lot of the old tunes from his Gran, and many more of the standards he'd learned from Mike, so they ended up having a sing-a-long. In his twenty minute break, an elderly gentleman offered to buy Ed a pint, and then sat down to join him. He was a nice enough chap and amusing company. He started to tell Ed of his own days as a musician, playing in a village brass band. Ed listened politely. He probably didn't have much of an audience these days for his tales, and it was better than sitting on his own. He confided in Ed that it was his first holiday alone, as his wife had passed on the year before. Sadly it was a tale that Ed had heard many times since he had been working in the coaching hotels. It was usually from the ladies however, and he hoped that his new friend wouldn't remain single for long.

After the gig, Ed felt a little more cheerful. He fetched the obligatory kebab from his favourite takeaway near the Triangle, and took it up to the car park to eat. It was only just past eleven and some of the gang were still around. Ed was thankful that he had shut his cowboy hat firmly in the boot with his shoelace tie and collar tips. Boy, that little lot would take some explaining! He got out of the car and brushed the pitta bread crumbs off his black jeans as he wandered over to see the others. Simon was there with a very pretty blonde, and seemed to have successfully removed a couple of small items of clothing. Brad also had a girl in the car, but apparently not with the same degree of success. They were both stony faced and obviously not speaking. Tony and Gary were both in similar hot-hatches, parked side by side as usual, talking through open windows. They were also joined by a bloke a little older than himself in a gold Mk1 Ford Capri. Ed had seen him around before, but didn't know his name. Nice car though! Gary, Tony and Brad all waved as he walked over but Simon seemed oblivious to anything going on outside his car, and who could blame him! Ed asked them all if they knew anything about Daz but no-one could recall seeing him for at least a week. They chatted and smoked for a while till Simon re-emerged and gave Ed a huge grin while his girlfriend made some hasty re-adjustments to her attire.

The cars all started up at once and he watched them roar away down the slope in convoy. He gave a wave as they all blasted on their horns, and turned back towards his own car with a smile on his face. It was a beautiful night with a full moon and hundreds of stars. For once there wasn't a breath of wind, and everything was peaceful and still, a perfect night for a walk along the beach.

Just before he reached the car he heard a shout. It was a female voice, scared, coming from the direction of the churchyard path.

"No! No!" Then after a few moments silence, "Get off me!"

Ed's blood ran cold and he had a dreadful feeling of deja-vu. Once again he found himself running across the car park and along the churchyard path. Once again he called out but got no answer.

He ran on down the hill, past the massive tomb, and into the churchyard itself. He ran on through the gates and into the road. There were several teenage girls hanging around, mainly in pairs or groups, but no-one in distress. He turned back towards the base of the church where a group of boys were sitting on the bench, and approached them desperately.

"Did any of you hear someone shouting?" They looked at him with dazed, bleary eyes. Ed tried again.

"Did anyone hear a woman shout?" He realized that they had probably been taking something, plus they were all holding cans of beer. A couple of them shrugged and one tried to focus his bloodshot eyes on him.

"Just mucking about," he said, then giggled. Ed turned away in disgust. This bloody place was getting on his nerves.

He started to stride back towards his car, when about half way up he heard the snap of a twig. He stopped and listened. Unlike the last time, there was no wind and the trees were silent, so that even small sounds were clear. Ed peered cautiously into the bushes, but could see nothing. He was just about to continue on his way, when a shape in the bushes to the left of him broke cover and tore off through the trees down the steep hillside. It scared the crap out of Ed and he shot back, muttering,

"Silly sod!" If people wanted to play silly buggers in dark churchyards at night, let them get on with it. He was going home.

As he walked away, there was another small sound behind him, a bit like a whimper. He wanted to ignore it, but resolutely turned back. It was most likely an injured animal of some sort.

He pushed his way into the bushes again, sighing deeply. A sharp bramble caught his arm and he swore. He ploughed on a little further, and there in front of him was another of those wretched stones. He could see that it was an old stone cross, its surface blotchy in the poor light, dappled with lichen and moss. He absently reached out and touched it, and then recoiled his hand suddenly, feeling something wet and sticky. He forced his way back to the feeble light of the path and looked at his fingers. It was blood!

A cold sickly feeling swept over Ed and he looked wildly around, hoping to see a passer by. No-one! He ran like a demon back up to his car where he grabbed his mobile phone, then rummaged wildly in his boot till he came up with a torch. He tore back to the spot and plunged into the bushes again, a mixture of rhododendron and vicious bramble. The beam from his torch was yellow and feeble, but it was enough. The stone cross had a solid square base, about a foot high, with some sort of engraved plaque on it. His heart was beating like a wild thing, and it was making him feel light headed. He pressed into the thicket and there in the light of his torch, poking out from behind the stone base were a pair of pale feet. He dropped to his knees and touched one. It was warm. He forced his head and shoulders into the holly bush, thrusting his torch in front of him, shouting to the still form and getting no response. The stiffly interwoven branches were forcing him back. He could just make out some long blonde hair, torn clothing and smudges of blood. He couldn't tell if she was dead or alive. Sobbing now, he returned to the path and dialled 999 on his mobile.

"I've found a body!"

The police were stationed outside the nightclubs down below, and were there in two minutes, and the ambulance followed in less than five. Someone had placed a blanket around Ed's shoulders and shepherded him into the back of a police car. He had watched them carefully move the girl into the open and start to apply first aid. The front of her body looked to be a mass of cuts and bruises, and there was a nasty gash on her head. One officer commented that she must have been literally thrown into the bushes, possibly catching her head on the stone cross as she went. Ed's heart wept to see the damage inflicted on this small, fragile form. She was clearly very young, and he felt a sudden surge of anger for the monster who could do this.

He was driven to the station, only a few hundred yards away, and found himself alone in an interview room facing a mug of sweet tea. Tea again! It was going to take more than bloody tea to put this right. He took a sip and tried to gather his thoughts. One of the officers from the scene entered the room and sat opposite him, and a few seconds later a younger one joined him.

"How is she?" Ed wanted to know.

"Well, she's alive," said the older man. "We won't know any more for a while but we'll keep you informed. Do you feel up to answering a few questions?"

"I'll do my best," replied Ed.

"How are you feeling?" he continued. He had thin grey hair and had a quiet, competent manner of speaking. Ed was grateful for his concern, but for a reason he couldn't put his finger on, he instinctively didn't trust him.

"I'll be fine when I've stopped shaking."

"Take your time. You've had a nasty shock. Just tell us, in you own words, everything you can remember."

"You see," added the younger one with feeling, "If he's on foot, and he has blood on him, he might still be in the area. We need to catch this bastard!"

The questions went on for ever, and Ed was frustrated at how little he could tell them. After about half an hour they took a break, and the older officer left the room for a few minutes. He had been told both their names at the beginning of the interview, but for the life of him couldn't remember them. When he returned, the questioning seemed to have taken a new turn, and it occurred to Ed that they considered him a possible suspect. He'd had enough! He couldn't think straight. He wanted to cry, he wanted to be someone else, somewhere else. He asked where the cloakroom was. The officer immediately looked at him in concern.

"Are you alright son?"

"Yeah," replied Ed. "I had a couple of pints earlier."

"Oh!" smiled the officer with sympathy, and gave him directions.

Ed reached the cloakrooms and shut the door behind him, grateful to be alone at last. He caught sight of himself in the mirror and got a shock. It was a wonder they hadn't arrested him straight off! His face looked deathly pale and his eyes were dark circles. There were small scratches all over his face, and deep ones down his left cheek and chin, oozing blood. His hair looked like nothing on earth, and still had bits of foliage in. He ran some water in the sink and tried to wipe most of the mess off his face. By some miracle his comb was still in his pocket, so he wet his hair and removed the debris, combing it flat.

There was a knock on the door and the younger officer entered.

"Are you OK, Ed?"

"Yeah, fine."

"Didn't you go to school in Wimborne?" he asked. Ed looked up in surprise, and really saw him for the first time.

"Bloody hell! Dave Walker!"

"Yep. P.C. Dave Walker to you mate."

"Bloody hell!" repeated Ed, and laughed. "How are you?"

"Better than you right now, I guess."

"Yeah, thanks."

"Look, I've had a word with the boss and he says you can go. Do you need a lift?"

"No thanks, I don't live far away. I could use some fresh air."

"Yes, I expect you could," he said wearily. "Look, I'm sorry about that. We have to cover every possibility you see. Being a mate of mine wouldn't cut much ice around here!" he added with a grin.

"I bet it wouldn't."

"Well, I'd better let you go then. I've got your details. Is it OK if I give you a call, let you know how the girl is? Maybe when this is over we should catch up over a pint," said Dave.

"That would be really good. I'll get off now then. See you."

"Yeah, and Ed? Take it easy mate!"

He somehow found his car and got it home. He walked through the door, went straight across to the bed and lay down in the dark, with only the light of a street lamp shining through the window. At last the tears came, spilling freely down both sides of his face onto the pillow and then, mercifully, he slept.

He woke next morning with a jolt to the sound of his mobile ringing. Damn! It was 9.15am and he had forgotten to set his alarm. It was Pearl and she didn't sound very pleased. He promised to be there in fifteen minutes and she rang off. He was still fully dressed but his clothes were ruined, and he quickly got changed and left without shaving. When he arrived she was standing in the doorway, hands on hips, wearing a long, bright red thing and matching lipstick. She looked like an angry letter box! When she saw his face her hands flew to her mouth and she started shouting hysterically.

"Oh my goodness gracious! You've been in an accident! Are you hurt? I knew something was wrong, I just knew it! Look at your beautiful face! Oh my poor baby!"

"Please Pearl, I'm all right," he said firmly. "Just let me through the door."

He told the Patels what had happened, and they listened to the local news together. The attack was headline news. The girl was named as Helen Parrott and she was seventeen years old.

She hadn't regained consciousness and her condition was described as critical. Police were appealing for help from the public and all information would be treated in the strictest confidence. Mrs Patel spent the day flapping and fussing, while Mr Patel looked very upset, and kept shaking his head and tutting with his tongue. They offered to let him go home, but he preferred to stay and have company.

Dave Walker phoned just before midday to say that Helen's condition hadn't changed and that she was in Poole hospital, soon to be transferred to Bournemouth. Ed wanted to visit her and Dave said that he would arrange it. Then he rang off, promising to phone again later. At three thirty, Mr Patel finally talked Ed into going home. He wandered back and turned on the telly, but found he couldn't concentrate. He felt cold and sore, so he went down the corridor to run a bath. He really liked the communal bathroom. It was quite a large room, about twelve foot square, and with a little imagination could really have been something. The huge old bath was white enamel over cast iron with claw feet. There was a trail of limescale in interesting shades of orange and green, running from the base of the huge brass taps to the plug hole. The sink was also massive and ornate, and the wall tiles were a lovely deep green glaze, similar to the ones on his fireplace. The ancient lino on the floor had a multi coloured pebble pattern and was stiff and curling at the edges. Ed lay deep in the pine scented bubbles and looked at the delicate tracery of the fine sculptured ceiling, feeling his aches and pains slowly melting away. This was the most comfortable bath he had ever used. This was also clearly the best time to use it. Most evenings he could hear people stomping up and down the corridor with their towel in their hand, muttering whilst waiting for their turn.

He hadn't forgotten Sharon, and when he returned to his room he could see that she had called his mobile while he was in the bath. He wasn't sure that he still wanted to go tonight, but he also didn't want to let her down. Reluctantly he dialled her number, and she answered almost straight away.

"Hello," she answered.

"Hi! It's Ed"

"Oh great! I've got some good news."

"What?"

"I've had a text from Daz. He says he's OK and he's in Southampton."

"Southampton? What's he doing there?"

"I don't know. That's all it says. 'Hi Mum. I'm in Southampton. Back soon.'"

"Oh! Not much point in us looking round Bournemouth then, is there?" said Ed.

"No, not much," she agreed. "Are you OK? You sound a bit down."

" I'm just having a bad day. Nothing to worry about."

"Want to tell me about it?" He hadn't meant to but he found himself telling her the lot.

"Oh my God! Are you all right? That's not just a bad day, it's a nightmare!"

"Let's hope I wake up soon then."

"What are you doing tonight? Why don't you come over here and let me cook you dinner," said Sharon. "No strings I promise. Its just that you've been so kind, and I love cooking. It's no fun just cooking for yourself. Please?"

"OK. No strings. I could do with some company. Thanks." As he closed his phone he wondered what it was that made strange women want to feed him. Did he really look that pathetic?

Chapter 6

Ed parked his car right outside Sharon's house, pleased to have found his way without resorting to the mobile phone. He had managed to sort out his appearance a little, though shaving had been a less than joyful experience. Deciding what to wear had been even worse.

He had put on his cream jeans and a long sleeved black shirt, but then caught his reflection in the mirror and decided it looked too formal. Then he had settled on his comfy old blue jeans and a grey T shirt, before deciding that he ought to make slightly more effort. He ended up in blue jeans and a snowy white shirt, wondering what on earth he was doing. For goodness sake! It wasn't as if he had to impress her! He stopped on route at a convenience store and grabbed a bottle of white wine. He looked briefly at the flowers, just to say thank you, but decided against it. Why the hell did he feel so nervous? Was it really that long since he'd had female company? What would he be like on a real date?

He walked up her path holding the bottle in front of him and feeling a little foolish. He took a deep breath as he knocked on the door. A good home-cooked meal and some company should be just what he needed. The door opened and there she stood in faded jeans and a soft blue T shirt. Their eyes met and he heard her sharp intake of breath as she saw his injured face. She reached up and gently touched his cheek. It was a strangely intimate gesture, and for a moment he was lost for words.

"Oh Ed," she gasped. "Are you OK?"

"Yes, I'm fine. Really," he said firmly. "Do I look that bad?"

"I'm sorry, do come in." she said, letting him past her into the hall. "You look nice, I mean……Oh God, let's have a drink!" Clearly she was feeling as nervous as he was. She took the bottle and went into the kitchen to fetch glasses while he went into the cosy lounge. He could hear her put his bottle in the fridge and take out one that was already chilled. He looked round the lounge, trying to get a feel for the people who lived here.

It was a nice room, a bit cluttered, with plain cream walls and a bright blue suite with yellow scatter cushions. She returned and waved him to sit down while she poured wine into two tall glasses. Ed chose an armchair while she sat on the sofa with her feet curled up next to her. Ed noticed with amusement that while her fingernails were bitten short, her toenails were a riot of colour, with stencilled flowers and palm trees, and she was also wearing several toe rings. Her first question was inevitable.

"Any news of the girl?"

"No. No change so far. I'm going to visit her as soon as they let me."

"Has she regained consciousness yet?"

"No. They tell me her condition is still critical. I'm lucky, I've got a mate on the force so they're keeping me updated."

"Good," she said. "That poor girl! Her parents must be out of their minds with worry. Sorry! I invited you round to forget about all that. Do you like pasta? I forgot to ask."

"Love it."

"Oh good! It won't take long." They both felt a little awkward at first, but as the wine began to flow, so did the conversation. There was no more news of Daz. Ed learned that Sharon worked the early shift at a newsagent, and she laughed openly as he told her all about the Patels and their funny little ways.

Dinner was simple but delicious, a tasty pasta dish with bacon and mushrooms in a tomato sauce served with garlic bread fresh from the oven, followed by a home-made apple crumble with cream. Sharon was a good cook and good company, and Ed found himself relaxing and enjoying himself. After dinner, and some more wine, they both ended up on the sofa.

"So!" said Ed with a grin. "Tell me about your toes." She unfolded her legs and wiggled her feet in front of him.

"Ah! My little vanity! Do you like them?"

"I'm not sure," replied Ed. "Do they make up for the fingers?"

"We won't talk about that." She hastily put her hands out of sight. "You're rotten."

"OK, I love your feet. They're interesting! Different! How am I doing?"

"Wow! Who taught you to grovel?" she replied. "They did a lousy job!"

"Actually," he confided, the wine loosening his tongue, "my wife taught me to grovel, and I think she did a very good job."

"Oh, so you're married. Should have guessed!"

"Why?"

"All the nice ones are married."

"Oh flattery!" he said pleased. "Actually we're separated."

"What happened?" she asked cautiously.

"Well! We were married for nine years, happily, or so I thought, and then she found someone else. You know," he said, attempting to lighten the mood. "Younger, better looking."

"Now that last bit I don't believe!"

"What, more flattery?" He said, with exaggerated disbelief.

"How long ago did it happen?" she asked.

"Last month." He replied, and hurriedly changed the subject. "And you?" She hadn't missed the flash of pain in his eyes, and immediately regretted being so nosey.

"Happily single!" she announced. "Have been on and off since Daz was fifteen."

"Daz told me you had a boyfriend."

"So, you've been checking up on me!" she teased. "What

else has Daz told you?" Ed remembered the rest that Daz had told him, and didn't feel like sharing it. He reflected that it was hard to believe they were talking about the same woman.

He settled for; "Well I don't think he was too keen on your last boyfriend!"

"Oh really? Les was alright. Completely unreliable though. Funny that! I thought Daz quite liked him. Thick as thieves they were sometimes. Les was always trying to get him to go out more. It was also Les who got him that job at the petrol station. I expect he's lost that now. He makes me so mad!"

"I expect it was hard being left to cope with him on your own."

"No, not really. He used to be a really easy kid. Then he became a teenager and I hardly ever saw him."

They carried on chatting for ages and he found himself telling her about his music. She sounded genuinely interested and said that she would love to see him play one day. He managed to laugh it off without actually inviting her, aware that his secret was finally out. She looked a little hurt at the implied rejection, and changed the subject quickly.

"Would you like some coffee?"

"Yes please, two sugars," he replied. " Then I'd better go and leave you in peace."

"Well I'm going to settle down and watch a film. You're welcome to join me."

"I won't if you don't mind, maybe another night. I'm really tired."

"Yes of course. Just the coffee then." Sharon took the hint, and told herself that it was early days. She couldn't help it. She found him fascinating. The way he looked directly into her eyes when he spoke, his endearing self-consciousness on one hand, and his easy confident manner on the other. A girl could really feel like someone with a bloke like Ed on her arm. Who was she kidding? He was young, free and single, good looking, and obviously on the rebound, while she was an older, dumpy, single mum who lived on a council estate! Time to get real and accept that he would only ever be a friend. One wrong move now and she would scare him away for ever, and she really didn't want to take that risk.

Next morning Ed skipped his run and decided to tidy the bedsit. He wasn't working today so he made some tea and pottered about for a while. He examined his face in the mirror, and decided that if anything, he looked worse. The deep scores down the side of his face had hardened and dried to an attractive black! He tried to gently sponge the crust off but it started to weep. Yum! Black and red! He decided it was best left alone. On a whim, he wrote a letter to his sister, and one to Anne. To Anne he wrote a newsy letter, and didn't mention the attack as he knew it would upset her. To Lara he wrote all his news, telling her about his gigs, his work at the shop, and about his role in the 'Helen' incident. He also passed on his mobile phone number. Although he and Lara had never been close, they liked to stay in touch, and writing to his sister had the added benefit of keeping his parents up to date, as he knew she still phoned them every Sunday.

Dave Walker rang at 9.30am.

"Hiya mate. How ya doing?"

"OK," replied Ed. "Any news?"

"Yes. Helen was moved to Bournemouth Hospital last night. That means they think she's out of danger, but she still hasn't regained consciousness yet."

"Is that normal?"

"Well, it's early days, but between you and me, the doctors are fearing some kind of brain damage. Nothing has been mentioned to the family yet, and they are still awaiting the results of a scan."

"When can I see her?" asked Ed.

"I'm going over this morning. Do you want me to pick you up?"

"No thanks. I can meet you there. What time?"

"I'll try and be in the reception at 11am, but you know what the job's like. If I'm not there, go out into the car park and call me on the mobile. You can't use it in the hospital."

"No problem," said Ed. "I'll be there."

Ed finished his letters and looked out the window. It was coming on to rain. He was going to go to the postbox, but changed his mind, and picked up his guitar. His agile fingers worked cleverly across the fretboard, and he was pleased with the way his latest song was taking shape. He had tried not to make this one morbid, but its theme became one of needing to cherish and protect those around him, and his strong emotions were inextricably weaved through each line of the haunting melody. As he wrote it, images of Helen's face floated before him, and he realized how important her survival had become to him. Also thoughts of Anne, and even Sharon were present, but interestingly, and for the first time, not Lisa. He realised that this simple song was becoming a mixture of all his hopes and dreams for the few people left that he cared about, and Lisa was no longer in there.

Ed had set up some simple recording equipment in his room, with his stereo and some old bits and pieces he had picked up in a second hand shop in Boscombe. He plugged it all together and switched it on, inserting an old fashioned tape cassette into the deck. He pulled up a chair and angled his microphone towards himself, then pressed the record button. He waited for five seconds to allow the tape to run on, then started to play. This time he closed his eyes and raised his voice, so that the sweet, haunting song would be captured at its best, all the time praying that the woman downstairs wouldn't start banging on the ceiling. When he had finished, he stopped the tape and rewound it, then played it back. As he expected, the quality was poor but it was all there, and even he had to admit to himself, he sounded good! He ejected the tape and put it down on the coffee table with a smile. What did it matter? No-one would ever get to hear his sad little tune! He checked his watch. It was ten thirty, so he quickly packed away his gear and left for the hospital. When he got there he had a bit of trouble finding a parking space, and drove round for a good five minutes before he finally saw someone pulling away. Bournemouth Royal Hospital was a fairly new building, its most outstanding feature being the bright blue roof. The main reception hall was a huge area, almost cut diagonally in half by a massive staircase. Bright pictures and murals decorated the walls, and the friendly aroma of coffee reminded Ed that he hadn't had any breakfast. All around him was orderly chaos; he had obviously arrived at a busy time. The well equipped coffee bar was tucked along one side of the stairway, and as he was still early, Ed bought himself a cup of coffee and a cherry muffin and sat at a table where he had a good view of the entrance.

Voluntary helpers waited nearby with welcoming smiles, ready to guide bemused visitors to their correct destinations, thus avoiding much chaos and confusion in the maze of corridors. Ed was full of admiration for them, and could appreciate what a vital roll they played in the smooth running of the hospital. Almost in the entrance itself was a shop unit selling just about everything, where people in all states of dress, from formal suits to nighties and pyjamas, were picking up sweets, newspapers and toiletries. Near to that was a florist, whose colourful displays brightened the entrance. The whole atmosphere of the place was friendly and welcoming, and one of constant activity. Not at all what one would expect from a hospital reception!

Ed drained his coffee cup and picked up the last few crumbs of his muffin. It was delicious! Keeping one eye on the door he made his way to the florist and selected a bunch of ten peach rosebuds, wrapped in spotted cellophane. The lady took his money and said that she hoped the receiver would like them. Ed just smiled blankly at her, wondering whether Helen would even get to see them. At once he felt nervous about the ordeal that lay ahead, and spun round, wondering if he shouldn't have come.

Then he saw Dave striding confidently towards him, a bright smile on his face.

"Sorry I'm late, Ed," he said, holding out his hand. "Had to see a man without a dog!" Ed shook his hand and they made their way to the ward, down seemingly endless miles of corridor.

"Thanks for coming with me," said Ed.

"That's OK. I have to get some background from the parents. Her mum won't leave her bedside, so I had to come anyway."

"What sort of background?"

"Well, we have to investigate the possibility that she knew her attacker, though I think that's unlikely in this case. I need to ask about threats of any sort, ex boyfriend problems, that sort of thing. You never know."

"I see," said Ed as they rounded the corner onto a ward. Ed hung back as Dave spoke to the sister on duty. Dave then beckoned Ed to follow, and they entered a ward with eight beds in two rows of four. Helen's was the last one on the right. Two women were sat by the bed, very similar in appearance, and once again Ed hung back as Dave went forward and took the hands of one of the women, speaking words of reassurance in a low, sympathetic voice.

All Ed could see of Helen was the tiny form in the large white hospital bed, surrounded by drips and tubes. Her pretty face was now unrecognisable, as the bruising and swelling had taken over in livid stripes of black and purple. Her long blonde hair had been bandaged back off her face and an ugly line of stitches and congealed blood ran along one side of her forehead. His heart went out to her, and he felt an urge to go to the bed and lift the tiny, lifeless hand from the sheet and hold it tight, willing some sort of life back into the still form.

Instead he just stood with his mouth open, until the sound of his name brought him back to the present. Dave had taken hold of his arm, firmly and reassuringly, seeing at once that Ed was still shaken.

"Ed," he said, "This is Mrs Parrott, Helen's mother." Ed

looked at the short, grey haired woman before him and held out his hand in greeting, unsure of the protocol of such an occasion. He was surprised at how old she was, possibly sixty. She must have had Helen very late in life. Dave continued speaking. "Mrs Parrott, this is Edward Curran, the man who saved your daughter."

She had obviously spent much time crying, but now fresh tears sprung to her eyes, and she let go of Dave's hand and reached for Ed's, her long nails digging into his flesh like claws.

"Oh Edward. How can I ever thank you?" Ed was completely unaware that he had been cast in the role of hero, and as a result, didn't know what to say. He looked to Dave for assistance, but Dave stood back, smiling at Ed's embarrassment, letting him take the praise that was his due. Ed glanced back at Helen and said,

"How is she Mrs Parrott?"

"The doctors tell us that she is stable, so that is good isn't it?" She looked at Ed, her eyes full of hope and desperation.

"Yes. That's very good," said Ed gently. Mrs Parrott spoke again.

"I want you to meet Lou, my sister." He solemnly shook hands with Lou, who looked him straight in the eye and said,

"Pleased to meet you." Although at first the two women had appeared similar, he could see now that Lou was a whole different ball game. Where the mother's eyes were soft and hopeful, Lou's were sharp, almost piercing. He immediately got the feeling that this woman was no fool, and that for some reason she was sizing him up.

"Pleased to meet you too!" he replied, looking directly back at her. It occurred to Ed that maybe she suspected him, as the police had clearly done for a short while. Well that was fair enough. Someone had done this family a great wrong, and Ed wasn't the only one who wanted to see justice.

He finally approached the bed and lay the rosebuds down on the cover. He gently took her delicate hand and spoke to her.

"Hello again Helen. Please get better, for all of us. I'm sorry I didn't get there sooner. If only I'd known. If only……" His voice finally cracked and tears started to run down his face. "I'm so sorry," he said, turning to Mrs Parrott. "Can she hear me?"

"We think so," she said reassuringly, "Don't we Lou?" Ed felt a hand on his shoulder and was surprised to see that it was Lou. She addressed Dave and her sister.

"I'm taking Edward for a cup of tea. I'm sure you two have things to discuss." She waited for Ed to follow her into the corridor, towards a restaurant that he'd never seen before. She opened her bag and silently handed him a tissue with a lipstick stain on it, and he thankfully re-folded the tissue and dabbed his eyes, trying to compose himself.

They queued up and then carried their mugs to a table in the far corner where no-one else was sitting. Ed looked out of the window, and was surprised at the number of gulls circling right outside. It was like looking through a kaleidoscope of grey and white, swooping and swirling through space, disorientating his senses. He gathered his thoughts, then turned his attention to the elderly woman sitting opposite him. He was disconcerted to find that she was staring hard at him again, and wondered what was coming next.

"Right, Edward!" she said briskly. "Drink your tea. You and I have a lot to talk about!"

Chapter 7

" **T**he thing is, I can read people's minds!"

"Sorry?"

"It's quite simple. I'm a mind-reader."

"Is that like a gift or something?"

"No. To be honest it's been more of a curse." Ed was getting out of his depth.

"Right!" he said. Lou took a deep breath.

"Edward?" she said, with a disconcertingly direct look. "Do you believe what you see with your own eyes?" She paused, choosing her words carefully. "Or do you prefer to go along with what others tell you? Are you simply a sheep? You see, people have been looking at me the way you are for most of my life. They require proof! They think I'm a crank!"

"OK, I'll be honest with you," said Ed. "I'm a sceptic! I've only just met you, but already I would believe that you are a very perceptive person. You size people up, see right through them, just as you were doing to me on the ward."

"I see I rattled your cage. I'm sorry. I do that a lot. It really is a curse you know. Give me your hand."

"What?"

"Do you want to find this bastard or not?" Ed was fast losing his grip on the conversation. He nodded dumbly at her.

"Edward! You are a sceptic! You require proof, and I need your help so I will give you proof. Now give me your hand!"

"OK," he replied, and held out his left hand across the table to her, glancing round uneasily to see if anyone was watching.

Lou held his hand tightly in both of hers and stared straight into his eyes. It was unnerving, and for a moment Ed had to fight the urge to laugh. She then bowed her head down, shutting her eyes, and pressed his hand to her forehead. They both sat there, not moving a muscle for a good twenty seconds. Then she spoke, still not moving or raising her head.

"You are a calm, contented person. You haven't seen much in your lifetime. You haven't travelled far. You have no great thirst for knowledge. I see no great ambition in you."

"Thanks! Any good news?"

"Oh yes. You are kind hearted, soft if you like! You are very protective of those you care about. You will not allow those around you to be hurt, but you will take it yourself and not fight back."

"Great! So I'm a coward too!"

"Oh no! You are very brave. And strong. Stronger than you know. I think you will need to be. Wait! You have lost something very dear to you. Or is it someone? Oh! Perhaps you've lost everything, and very recently!" Her eyes flew open and she looked at him with concern. "Oh my poor Edward!" Ed was shaken but kept his head.

"Go on. I'm not helping you," he said levelly. She looked at him scornfully and resumed her position.

"There is a new passion in your life. It's not a person, though. There are lots of happy faces looking at you. I'm sorry but things come through in bits and pieces. You have to be patient! There is a party somewhere and everyone is looking at you. Are you an entertainer or a musician? It's all very confusing. How am I doing?"

"Anything else?" asked Ed, fascinated. He received another dirty look!

"You seem to be going through a period of huge change. You are all at sea, drifting if you like, like a ship who's lost its anchor and is prepared to go where the wind blows it. I also see betrayal. Not just one but maybe two or three. Yes. I see that you have been betrayed in some way by those closest to you, but instead of staying and fighting you have simply cut free. In my experience that takes a lot more guts. You have kept your pride in tact, that's always important!" She looked up at him and smiled. "Oh my dear boy, you are in a pickle! Well, what do you think?" Ed gulped and looked back at her, eventually finding his voice.

"I think, that if you ever get to meet this bastard, you will know."

They finished their tea, and then Ed asked her the question he had been longing to ask.

"You said you wanted my help?"

"Ah, yes! I want you to take me to where it happened. I want to get a feel of the place."

"Why?"

"I'm not sure, I just need to. Perhaps I might be able to get the feel of the person who did it. It usually only works on people, not places, but it has to be worth a try. I know that no-one would listen to an old dear like me, even if I did learn something, but I need to try, for Helen,.....for me."

"I would listen to you," said Ed.

"Thank you Edward."

"And please don't call me Edward, you sound like my mother. Call me Ed."

"Ah yes, your mother! And we don't want to go there, do we?"

"Not right now thanks. Yes, I would be pleased to take you there. When would you like to go?"

"We can go now if you're not busy," replied Lou.

"Why ask? You know everything else about me," he said darkly. She ignored the jibe and he continued. "Won't your sister miss you though?"

"Oh Mary? Yes, probably, but I can't do the sitting around in hospitals bit. I need to be out and about, doing something useful. I'm no good at tea and sympathy, holding hands and all that rubbish. I suppose you think I'm being unkind?"

"Do you really need to ask me what I think?" asked Ed.

"Now your pulling my leg!" she glared at him, then laughed. "I like you, Ed."

"Well I'm glad about that," he said. "I sure wouldn't want you for an enemy!"

This time Ed parked on the road near the church gates, and they walked up together through the churchyard. It all looked very different in daylight. Lou was wearing stout walking shoes, and had pulled on a dark green fleece over her fine lambswool jumper and sensible tweed skirt. About half way up on the left, he pointed into the brush and said,

"That's where I found her!" Lou peered into the bushes, then looked all around her, before speaking.

"Good Lord, what a place!"

"Yes! Isn't it! Well if you don't get weird vibrations here, you're just not trying."

"Thank you Ed but that's not helpful. Now where did you say you were standing?"

"Just here on the path, when I heard a small noise, like a sigh or a gasp."

"So what happened next?"

"I came back and tried to see into the bushes. I think I expected to see an injured animal or something."

"And just what did you see?" asked Lou. Ed cast his mind back and tried to repeat the sequence of events, speaking hesitantly as it came back to him.

"I saw the stone cross. It was dark and it gave me the creeps. I reached out and touched it; I'm not sure why. It was wet. I went back into the light and saw blood on my fingers. I ran back up to my car and fetched a torch and my phone. When I came back I shone my torch round the base of the stone and saw Helen's feet. I tried to see more but the torch was so weak and the bushes were too thick." Ed stopped talking and watched as Lou stomped about in the undergrowth.

"Damn!" she said. "I've laddered my tights." He watched her prowling both sides of the path till she came to a stop next to a large stone sarcophagus.

"This is where he waited for his victim," she said, putting her hand on the stone and closing her eyes, frowning. She stepped behind the stone and bobbed down, so that only the top of her grey curly hair was visible. Ed remained silent as she did her stuff.

"He was here, I'm sure of it. Anyway, look around. It's the only sensible place to hide. I keep seeing a shape. It makes no sense! I think it's a square; a small dark square."

"Anything else?" asked Ed.

"Well, maybe a circle." She reappeared, looking a little disillusioned. " Oh! I don't suppose it means anything," she said, shaking her head. She looked round her again and started walking up towards the car park.

"What the hell was Helen doing out here in the middle of the night?"

"Well there were a lot of people about, and the clubs were still busy down below. It's not as deserted as you might expect," said Ed.

"And what, if you don't mind me asking, were you doing here alone at that time of night?"

"Eating a kebab actually. I know it sounds silly but I had just finished work and I didn't want to go straight home to an empty flat, so I came up here for some piece and quiet."

"Yes. I can see that. Just eating and thinking," she said. "Winding down before bed!"

"Yes!" laughed Ed, "that's exactly how it was!"

"So where was she going?"

"I don't know." Lou suddenly turned towards Ed and said,

"I want to go back to the hospital now. Would you mind taking me?"

"No. that's fine!"

They turned together and headed back through the stone gates and down along the path towards the car. On the way home, Ed said to Lou,

"Tell me about Helen." Lou rummaged around in her purse for a second and came up with a dog-eared photo. Ed glanced down at it whilst he was driving, waiting for her to speak. The girl in the photo looked about twelve, and was wearing a stripey jumper and cuddling a dog. She looked as though butter wouldn't melt in her mouth!

"She has a face like an angel, doesn't she? Well she isn't; far from it! Mary was thirty six when she married Dennis. They both wanted children but nothing happened. Then after seven years, along came Helen! It was like a miracle. My sister was the happiest woman alive!" Lou was smiling at the memory. "Consequently, Helen was spoilt rotten! Broke her mother's heart when she developed a mind of her own. We never knew where she went or what she was up to. Her mother and father lost many a good nights sleep. Funny though; I always thought she was fairly streetwise. I guess at her age you think nothing can touch you."

"Anything else?" asked Ed, desperate for information.

"Well, she has a soft heart, and was always crazy about animals. I told Mary she should let her have a dog, but they wouldn't hear of it. Didn't want the noise and the mess! The dog in the picture was the neighbour's. Helen walked it most days after school. Ugly looking thing but she loved it. I can't remember it's name."

When they got back to the ward, Mary was with a tall man in a grey suit, who she introduced as Mr Parrott, Dennis. Ed shook hands again and asked if there was any change in Helen. Dennis Parrott shook his head and squeezed his wife's hand. Mary's eyes brimmed with tears again, and they resumed their silent vigil, side by side on the metal chairs next to Helen's bed. Dave had clearly left a while ago, and Lou stood next to Ed, the two of them feeling like spare parts.

Lou finally broke the silence by addressing her sister.

"Mary. Would you mind if I sat with Helen for a moment?"

"Of course!" Mary replied eagerly. "Do you think you could get through to her?" Mary Parrott looked up at Ed. "My sister is psychic, you know!" she said proudly.

"Now don't get carried away," said Lou sternly. "It doesn't always work." She took Helen's left hand in her right one, and lay her other hand against the lifeless girl's cheek, staring with concentration at the still face. Her expression reminded Ed obscurely of his mother, trying to read small print without her glasses. No-one moved. It seemed as though no-one breathed. After a minute or so a frown crossed Lou's face, then a puzzled expression. Unable to contain herself any longer, Mary spoke up.

"What is it?" she demanded. Lou looked up and shook her head.

"I'm sorry," she said. "I can't seem to concentrate. I'm sure she knows we're here, and doesn't want you to worry, but it's very faint. I think I'm just too tired. I'm sorry," she said again.

"No!" said Mary. "That's good isn't it?" She looked eagerly at her husband. He squeezed her hand and gave her a smile, then went back to staring at his daughter, obviously unimpressed by Lou's performance.

Ed spoke to Lou.

"If you're tired, I can give you a lift home."

"No thank you Ed. I'll get a taxi a bit later. No need for you to stay though. Come on, I'll see you out."

Ed said goodbye to the tragic couple, and left the ward with Lou at his side.

"OK," he said, now they were alone at last. "You saw something. What was it?"

"I'm not sure. It's very strange. I need a piece of paper." She rummaged through her bag, and came up with a tatty envelope, the one that had contained Helen's photo, and a pencil stub. She held the envelope flat against the wall of the corridor and started to draw. Then she handed it to Ed. On the envelope, Lou had drawn a square, about four inches across. In the centre of the square she had drawn a circle, just over an inch in diameter.

"It's the same symbol as I saw earlier. Does it mean anything to you?"

"No," said Ed, handing it back.

"No, me neither. I'm probably losing it!"

"Are you sure you'll be OK here?"

"Yes. I want to make sure they get something to eat before I go. Otherwise they won't bother, and they are going to need all their strength."

"OK. Goodbye then Lou."

"Goodbye Ed; and thank you!"

And that was the first time that Ed met Louisa Dodds!

When Ed arrived home he realized that it was nearly tea time, and the muffin was all he'd had all day. He found two messages waiting for him when he switched his mobile back on. One was from Pearl and the other from Sharon, both wanting to know how Helen was. He called them both back and informed them that there was no change, but that her life was out of danger. They both made him promise to keep in touch. It was a good feeling to have people checking up on him, and it helped to keep the loneliness at bay.

Today was Thursday. He was playing a solo gig tonight, and again on Saturday as a duo with Mike. He realized that he hadn't spoken to Mike and Trish all week, so he gave them a call. Mike was working late so Trish answered the phone as usual, and he gave her all his news. She was shocked when she heard that it was Ed who had found Helen Parrott, and said that she would get Mike to call him when he got home. She asked if he wanted to come over for dinner that night with the family, but Ed explained that he was playing.

Trish was relieved that Ed wouldn't be on his own. For all his happy-go-lucky ways, she knew that he was really sensitive inside, and that this would have upset him deeply. In the short time that he had been in their lives, Sharon had become increasingly fond of Ed. Not only did she fancy him rotten, as did most women, but she felt strangely protective of him, almost maternal. She could see that he had also done wonders for her husband, for although Mike had the lion's share of both the musical ability and experience, he was no front man, bless him. Where Ed was clearly an extrovert, Mike was quiet and introverted. Ed seemed to thrive on the attention and the excitement, while Mike enjoyed the satisfaction of a job well done. For this reason, people always approached Ed with enquiries or requests, naturally assuming that he was the leader.

In fact it was usually Trish who dealt with agents and bookings by phone. It was a role she enjoyed, and she took a lot of the responsibility off the men, which suited them both down to the ground. There were contracts to be signed and returned, payments to be chased, and cheques to be banked and split on an almost weekly basis. If only Ed wasn't on his own! He seemed so young and vulnerable, and for the fiftieth time she cursed the woman who had ruined his life. Not naturally a match maker, Trish found herself mentally running through her list of friends, just wishing there was someone out there who really deserved him.

Hunger drove Ed up to the Patel's shop. Mr Patel was sat at the counter, reading a magazine, and he looked up as he came in.

"Ahh Edward, how are you?"

"Fine thank you. I've just come in for some shopping."

"And how is the young girl?"

"The same I'm afraid. No change yet but the doctors seem

hopeful."

"Ah yes. My wife tells me you have seen her. You are a kind man Edward."

Before Ed could respond, Pearl entered and rushed over and gave Ed a hug, one beaded earring nearly forced into his mouth!

"Hello, Mrs. P."

"Eddie! How are you? I have kept something for you." She delved into the deli counter, rounding on her husband as she did so. "Why didn't you tell me he was here?" She turned back to Ed, as Mr. Patel shook his head and went back to his magazine. "I have saved this for you Eddie. It is out of date but I know it's your favourite, so I didn't want to throw it away." Ed unwrapped the paper bundle she had placed in his hands and peered in. It was a large homity pie, and clearly a fresh one.

He could smell the garlic and the cheese, and it made his mouth water. He was about to protest when she glared at him and shook her head.

"Thank you so much, but you must let me pay for it!"

"No Edward. I told you, it would only be thrown away!"

"Well, thanks Pearl." Mr. Patel started tutting and shaking his head again. Ed gave them both a farewell and beat a hasty retreat with his spoils.

Mr. Patel bought in the homities from a local baker, and they were a firm favourite with many of their customers. The thought of one being left over was practically unheard of, and Ed had to smile at her generosity as he cut into the deep, gooey pie, sitting in front of the telly to eat it. It was just what the doctor ordered, and although it would be better warmed up, Ed just couldn't wait. The wonderful flavours of cheese, onion, garlic and buttery pastry filled his mouth, and Ed was all but swooning as he demolished over half the family sized pie. When he had washed it down with a mug of hot sweet tea he sat, full and contented, in front of the telly and contemplated what a wonderful woman Pearl was. After a while he looked at his watch and sighed. It was time to start getting ready for the gig.

On Friday, Ed had to work all day at the shop. The Patels went shopping soon after he arrived. Pearl left him with a mug of coffee and a Danish pastry, and he made the most of the peace and quiet, sitting at the counter with his feet up on the stack of baskets and reading a car magazine.

The day passed pleasantly enough. He did some dusting and some filling up, and as usual, it got busier around lunch time. He was pleased to see Sharon come into the shop, half an hour before he was due to leave. Mr. and Mrs. Patel had arrived back an hour earlier, and were watching the telly together. Ed had had no-one to talk to for the last twenty minutes, and was pleased to see a friendly face.

"Hiya gorgeous!" he grinned.

"Hello. I thought I'd found the right place," she replied.

"What you doing here?" asked Ed in surprise.

"It's my day off. I got bored with being in so I thought I'd have a look round the shops."

"Get anything nice?"

"No. Couldn't afford anything I liked, and didn't like anything I could afford. Usual story!"

"Oh. You'll have to let me take you shopping one day. I'll even buy you lunch, in return for the other night."

"Blimey! Do you mean it?" she cried.

It was funny. Ed hadn't even realized he was making the offer till he'd done it. All the same, the look on her face made him glad he'd asked. It was the sort of thing he'd done with Lisa fairly often.

"Of course I do! I quite like shopping. You might find I'm a bit out of touch though."

"Don't worry!" she laughed. "I'll be gentle with you! What time do you finish here?"

"About four o'clock," he replied. "Are you still going to be around?"

"I can be. Why?"

"It's going to be a nice evening. I really fancy a walk down the beach."

"That sounds nice. Can I wait with you?"

"Sure. You might be interrogated by Mrs. Patel when she finds I've got a woman in the place though!" said Ed dryly.

Sure enough, in came Pearl. She looked at the pair of them and put two and two together, making twenty five!

"Ah Eddie, you have a lady friend. Am I to be introduced?" She beamed brightly at him.

"Of course! This is my good friend Sharon. Sharon, this is my boss, Mrs. Patel."

"Call me Pearl," she purred taking Sharon's hand. "Everyone else does."

"Pleased to meet you Pearl."

"And how do you two know each other?" Pearl continued. Ed rescued her.

"I know Sharon's son," said Ed. "He works at the garage where I take my car."

"Golly gosh!" said Pearl to Sharon. "You have a son who is old enough to work. That makes you at least?..........."

"Thirty five," said Sharon.

"And do you work Sharon?"

"Yes. I work in a newsagents."

"Oh, which one? I might know it."

"The one on Stanton Street."

"And where do you live?"

"Pearl!" interrupted Ed. "Give the girl a break!" Pearl tried to adopt an injured expression.

"I'm only trying to show an interest in your friends. Just tell me if I'm in the way."

"Don't worry, Pearl," said Sharon. "I'll try and teach him some manners for you."

Ed gave up, knowing full well when he was out-numbered.

It was going to be a beautiful evening, and a little while later, Sharon and Ed were walking barefoot along the sand, carrying their shoes by the laces. The tide had left ribbons of seaweed and piles of stones dotted along the shoreline, and Sharon stopped to pick up shells every few paces. She turned a pink slipper shell over thoughtfully in her hands and spoke.

"I don't get down here nearly often enough. I'd forgotten how beautiful it is." The wind was ruffling her short blonde hair and her blue eyes shone with contentment. She was wearing her pedal pushers again, and the small, foamy waves splashed around her ankles.

"I try to get down here in the mornings before work. It's deserted then, except for a few mad joggers like me," said Ed.

"It sounds lovely, but I think I'd be too lazy to manage that. It's all I can do to crawl to work most mornings!"

"Oh, I think I could get you running," said Ed.

"How would you do that?" she replied.

"Like this!" he shouted, and ran into the sea, turning and kicking water all over her. She gasped with shock and ran at him to return the favour. Ed ran away at full speed through the ankle deep water, with Sharon madly chasing after him, both of them getting soaked to the skin. After a minute Ed slowed and turned. Sharon stopped and looked at him, panting hard. She leant her hands on her knees to get her breath back, calling him something unrepeatable.

"There you are!" he laughed. "I tell you what. You need to get fit!"

"Oh!" she said. "When I catch you!......."

"And how are you going to do that?" he replied.

"Just look at me!" she complained, silently dripping into the sand. Ed couldn't help grinning at her.

"Oh dear!" said Ed. "I would offer to take you home but I'm just too busy."

"Well, they won't let me on the bloody bus!"

They ended up laughing, and walking for miles with the

gentle breeze blowing through their wet things, drying them out but chilling them to the bone. When they finally got back to the pier approach, the smell of hot-dogs from a stall reminded them how hungry they were, and they sat side by side on the steps, looking out to sea, with steaming hot-dogs and paper mugs of tea. The gulls circled wildly above them, and Ed rolled his bread into pellets and was throwing them into the air. The screeching of the seagulls was deafening as they caught the bread, twisting, turning and diving in mid- air, making Sharon laugh with delight. When they had finished, Ed took her home, the two of them laughing and chatting all the way. She asked him to stop at the local store for some milk so she could make some coffee when they got in. Sharon opened the front door with her key, and stopped with surprise in the hall. A tatty black coat was hanging from the end of the bannister.

"Daz?" she shouted, and looked into the lounge. "Daz?" She turned to Ed and said, "Just a minute," before running up the stairs. Ed heard her talking to someone for a moment, then she reappeared at the top of the stairs.

"Is he OK?" asked Ed.

"Yeah, I think so." She looked both uncertain and relieved.

"Don't worry. I'll let myself out," said Ed.

"I'm sorry. Is that OK?"

"Of course," he smiled. "You see to Daz."

Ed let himself out of the front door, and walked down the path. He badly wanted to talk to Daz; the little runt had some explaining to do. However, now was clearly not the time, and he was glad that Sharon didn't have to worry any longer. The best thing he could do now was to leave them alone. He sat in the car for a moment and reflected on the last couple of hours. Sharon was certainly good company. He hadn't laughed so much in ages! He wondered what had possessed him to splash her like that. Lisa would have killed him!

Ed started the engine and pulled away. As he did so he was

aware of a figure sitting in the car behind him, only just visible as the windows were tinted. Alarm bells rang in his head. He drove to the end of the road, did a U-turn and passed the car again, trying not to make it obvious that he was looking. Sure enough there was the outline of a man in the driving seat, watching the house. The car was a white Ford Mondeo.

Chapter 8

Ed drove home deep in thought. He was almost certain that the white car was the one he had seen on the night of Daz's disappearance, but it looked like Daz was home again now, safe and sound. As he drove his mobile started to ring. He immediately swerved in towards the pavement and pulled up, afraid that Sharon was in some kind of trouble. He grabbed his phone, only to see that it was Mike's name on the caller display, probably checking the details for tomorrow night.

"Hello mate," said Ed. "Wha'sup?"

He was right. Mike gave him the place and time of the next gig and Ed promised to be there. Then he heard Mike hand the phone to Trish. She asked if Ed had any plans for Saturday daytime, and did he want to come out for a picnic in the forest with the girls? Ed thanked her and said that he would be round to theirs by 10.30am. It sounded fun. He folded up his mobile and headed towards Boscombe on his way home. In Boscombe he parked up and found a late store selling a wide variety of toys and gifts. When he came out ten minutes later he was carrying a pink football and a plastic bat and ball set in a net bag. He popped them into his boot and then drove towards the hospital.

Mary and Dennis Parrot were exactly where he had left them two days earlier. Only the change of clothes proved that they had ever been away. Ed silently approached the bed. Helen looked worse than ever. Her bruises were turning yellowish round the edges, the range of colours on her face now including greens, purple and black so that her own delicate features were drowned. She too had been changed into a fresh pale blue cotton nightie.

Mary Parrott looked up as he approached, and rose to meet him. Ed found himself holding both her hands and talking to her in the manner he had so admired when he had first seen Dave do it. Now it was natural, instinctive. Dennis rose briefly to shake his hand, then sat down heavily again. Ed wondered whether Dennis, as others had done, lay any of the blame for his daughter's state at Ed's door. But looking at the droop of his shoulders, the dullness of his eyes, his whole demeanour, Dennis looked like a man who had lost interest in everything. His whole reason for living was at this moment concentrated in the stark white bed before him, and with every passing day, she was fading away before his eyes.

Ed asked if he could fetch them a coffee or tea. Mary said that it was very kind of him but they had just had one. He looked around and saw the two mugs at their feet, still full but cold and scummy. Mary told him that Lou had been over in the morning, and had forced them to have lunch with her in the canteen. They had made the nurse promise to call them immediately if there was any change in Helen. Ed was surprised to hear that Dave had also visited, though only briefly. He made his mind up to call Dave as soon as he got in, and find out if there were any leads yet. Someone had put Ed's rosebuds in a vase, and they had opened into perfect little peach flowers. Once again Ed prayed that Helen would get to see them. There was no conversation to be had so Ed pulled up a chair and sat in silence with the Parrotts for ten minutes before quietly melting away. When he came out it was getting dark and there were fewer people around. Ed went home feeling lonely and dispirited. He finished off the pie and watched telly till bedtime, looking forward to tomorrow and his day in the forest.

Ed was wakened at 3am by the sound of his mobile ringing.

He sat up in fear, completely disorientated for a moment, then suddenly leapt out of bed towards the coffee table, where his mobile continued to ring. It was Dave.

"Ed! Can you get down here? Now? It's happened again!"

"Yeah, sure. What's happened?"

"Look, they wanted to come and find you but I insisted on calling you first."

"Why? What's going on?"

"Just get here will you? I'll explain then."

"OK!"

"And Ed?"

"Yeah?"

"It's bad!"

Ed closed his mobile, his heart beating wildly.

It took less than five minutes to drive to the police station, where he parked right outside. Dave came out to meet him and took him straight into the back. There were two more officers waiting for him in the interview room, only one in uniform. They waved him into a seat. Dave still hadn't told him anything. The plain-clothed officer spoke first.

"Thank you for coming in so promptly. I am D.I. Bateland, this is P.C. Warren. Dave Walker I understand you already know. I don't know how much you've been told." He glanced up at Dave who almost imperceptibly shook his head. "I'll start by asking you where you were tonight between midnight and 2am."

"In bed asleep," replied Ed.

"Any witnesses?"

"No, none."

"Anyone see you arrive home?"

"No. One of the neighbours may have heard me. The lady downstairs has hearing like a bat!"

"OK, we can check on that," said the officer. "Would you like some tea?"

"Thank you," said Ed. "Would you mind telling me what's going on?" Bateland looked long and hard at Ed before speaking, and when he finally spoke his eyes never left Ed's face.

"There has been a murder." Ed went rigid with shock. Bateland continued. "A nineteen year old girl was attacked in the early hours of this morning by a someone with a knife. She was found alive but died from her injuries on her way to hospital. We believe she was also hit over the head with a heavy object, though it's too early for any details. Anyway, she never regained consciousness."

"Where did this happen?" asked Ed, having already guessed the answer. He was wrong!

"Bourneside Park."

"Bourneside Park?" repeated Ed. "So what has this got to do with me?"

"We believe that this is the third attack by the same man. This murder took place only yards from the scene of the first attack. There are similarities between all three, though each one has been more serious than the last. The first one that we know of was the attack on Kelly Foster."

"I remember hearing about that on the radio a couple of weeks ago," said Ed.

"That's right," said Bateland. "Unfortunately Kelly didn't get a good look at the man, but he spoke to her, so she might recognise his voice. The second, as you know, is Helen, and our third victim is dead. Apart from Kelly Foster, you are our only witness."

"Am I also your only suspect?"

"Not really," said Bateland wearily. "As you can appreciate, it helps to know exactly where everyone was at the time of a murder. I regret that we will have to double check your whereabouts. I wouldn't be doing my job if I didn't."

"Fair enough!" said Ed.

The promised tea arrived. They all had a breather while it was given out. Then the balding man who had interviewed Ed the last time appeared at the door, and beckoned Warren and Bateland to come outside, leaving him alone with Dave.

"What's going on?" asked Ed.

"I don't know!" replied Dave, looking worried. "That's Mercier; he's a bastard. He's probably been getting it in the ear because we've got no leads on the Helen Parrott case. I hope he's not going to start on you. If he is, then I'll be taken off the case. Look mate, if he does start, just play it cool. They haven't got anything. He's a tricky sod though." And with that the door opened, and Mercier entered with P.C. Warren. Dave was told to leave.

Now it was just the three of them, and a whole new ball game started. Mercier switched the recorder on and got straight down to business.

"So Mr. Curran. Here we are again!" Ed didn't like his tone. "What's going on?" he demanded.

"I thought you'd been told. There's been a murder."

"And what's that got to do with me?"

"Well let's look at it shall we? This is the third attack that we know about. We know that you were very close to the scene of the first one. Your car was caught on CCTV just before it happened."

This was news to Ed, and he suddenly felt a chill all over. "We know that you were at the scene of the second one, and for the third one it seems that you have no alibi. It doesn't look very good, does it Mr. Curran?"

"OK, put like that, it doesn't," said Ed in desperation. "But you can't have found any proof because there isn't any."

"How do you know what we'll find? Something you're not telling us, Mr Curran?"

"No!" shouted Ed. "I know because it wasn't me. Look! I'm not having this. I'm innocent! I want to see somebody!"

"No point shouting for your mate Dave now. He's been assigned to another case." So Dave was right! He forced himself to remember Dave's words and calmed down. 'Stay cool'!

"I came here tonight voluntarily, and I think I'd like to go now."

"But we haven't finished with you yet, Mr. Curran. We need to establish exactly where you were tonight."

"And I've told you. I was alone in bed!"

"And I've told you! We need proof!"

"Look! I don't think you can force me to stay, can you?"

"We could always arrest you!"

"Well, you'd better do it then because I'm leaving!" Mercier sighed and turned to Warren.

"OK officer. You'd better read him his rights."

Ed was deep in shock as he was lead to the cells. Mercier lead the way, looking pleased with himself, while Warren walked beside him. He was taken to a desk where the custody sergeant made him turn out his pockets. At the sight of his mobile phone he asked if he could make a call. Mercier agreed, but told him to be quick. Ed found Mike's number and rang it. Mikes phone was switched off. In desperation he asked for a phone book and found their home number. On the ninth ring, Mike's sleepy voice answered. Ed quickly told him where he was and why. Mike said he would be straight over. Ed was then taken to a bare cell, and the door clanged shut behind him. Mercier had promised to return when Ed felt more like talking.

About an hour passed. Ed was lying on the narrow bunk, staring up at the ceiling in anger in the dismal, smelly cell, listening to a drunk ranting further down the corridor. He could hear someone mopping up what had looked like vomit outside his door. This was so unfair. He almost wished he had just kept on walking on the night when he found Helen, but he wasn't quite that hard hearted. Even now, he may have saved her life, though that was looking less and less likely. If only she'd wake up. That alone would make all this worth while. Also she could probably tell the police that Ed wasn't her attacker. At that moment, Helen's survival seemed like his only hope.

He did have another hope, who was at that moment powering along the corridor towards Ed's cell. She had made short work of the desk sergeant and then the custody sergeant, and had managed to talk her way into being allowed access to Ed. Before kids, Trish had been a legal secretary in a top flight firm of solicitors. She had in fact been personal secretary to the criminal defence solicitor, and Trish knew her onions! It hadn't taken much to persuade Mike that she was the man for the job, and that he should stay at home with the kids.

The hatch in Ed's door opened for a second and a face peered in. Then the door was unlocked and Trish entered with the custody sergeant. She went straight up to Ed and gave him a hug and a peck on the cheek.

"Are you alright?" she asked anxiously.

"Yes. I'm OK. Where's Mike?"

"At home with the kids. Don't worry, I'm going to get you out as soon as I can."

"How? I'm their prime suspect!"

"Trust me! I've done this before." The sergeant told her she'd have to leave. She looked at Ed and smiled. "Believe me! I'm more useful to you than Mike right now."

"Thanks Trish. Don't be long!" The door clanged shut again.

After a few minutes he could hear raised voices, one of whom was definitely Mercier, sounding rattled. A few minutes later the door opened and they were all lead to another interview room. As they were walking, Trish spoke to Ed in a low voice.

"Leave this to me." They all sat down and Mercier started by addressing Ed, his manner a little more formal than before.

"Mrs Walsh informs me that she is your legal representative. Is that correct?"

"Yes," replied Ed.

"Right! I'll ask you again. Where were you this morning between the hours of midnight and two?"

"I've told you," replied Ed. "I was asleep in bed. On my own!"

"I believe my client has already answered the question to the best of his ability. Could we move on?" asked Trish.

"OK. What sort of car do you drive Mr Curran?"

"A red BMW convertible."

"And where was your car at precisely 1.55am on Sunday, August the 15th?"

"Driving through Bournemouth I expect. I finished work at about half past one."

"Exactly right, Mr Curran. Your car was seen in Bournemouth town centre at exactly the time of the attack on Kelly Foster!" he said triumphantly.

"With respect," interrupted Trish, "that only proves that both Kelly Foster and Edward Curran were in the same town at the same time. It's hardly surprising since Mr Curran both lives and works there. Do you have anything a little more concrete ?"

"We are pursuing several lines of enquiry, Mrs Walsh."

"Do you have any evidence at all against my client?" Mercier looked down and steepled his fingers on the desk. He finally spoke.

"May I remind you that this is a murder enquiry, and we can afford to leave no stone un-turned." Trish responded immediately.

"And you won't find the culprit sat in here harassing innocent members of the public. May I remind you that my client came here voluntarily to assist......." and Trish continued her onslaught, throwing in expressions like 'circumstantial evidence,' 'wrongful arrest,' and 'victimisation!'

A few minutes later, Trish marched Ed out of the front entrance of the police station, with her head held high. She turned towards Ed, her eyes sparkling.

"God, I enjoyed that!" she announced. "Of all the arrogant, pompous, stupid…. Sorry Ed. Are you all right?"

"I think so," he replied. "How the hell did you do that?"

"I haven't always been just a mum you know."

"You'll never be 'just' a mum!"

Trish waited in the bedsit while Ed grabbed some clean clothes and stuffed them into a carrier bag. He wanted to shower but Trish insisted he did it at her house, so he made do with washing his face and brushing his teeth. She told him to leave his car at home and they would both go in hers. He just remembered to grab the toys out of the boot before they left.

When they got there, Mike was waiting up and had the kettle on ready. He gave Trish a quick kiss and shook Ed warmly by the hand.

"Are you OK, mate?" he asked.

"Yeah. I am now." Mike made the tea without asking any more questions; it wasn't his way. He handed round the steaming pottery mugs and lead the way into the lounge. The antique mantle clock was ticking loudly, and Ed was surprised to notice that it was almost six o'clock. He leant back in the deep squashy sofa and gave a sigh. Trish shut her eyes and sipped her tea. Mike broke the silence and asked if anyone was hungry. Ed smiled and told him that Trish had already eaten! Mike turned to her and raised his eyebrows in a silent question. She just smiled back, knowingly.

"OK! I'm almost afraid to ask," said Mike, "but is anyone going to tell me what the hell is going on?"

For the next half hour both Ed and Trish told the story, while Mike listened intently, asking only the occasional question. Suddenly a small ginger haired whirlwind in pink pyjamas entered the room, and leapt onto Mike. Another one walked in and curled up next to her Mum on the sofa. Soon Trish had one each side, snuggling up to her, and peeping shyly at Ed. He looked at the two identical freckled faces, with their mops of curly hair and said,

"How do you tell them apart?"

"It's quite easy," said Mike. "You just call them both 'pest' and they answer!"

"Daddy!" yelled two voices. One of them looked solemnly

at Ed and said,

"I'm Danielle but you can call me Danny, and this is my sister, Sophie! Did you sleep here?"

"No, I slept at the police station!" replied Ed seriously.

"Are you a policeman then?" asked Sophie shyly.

"No, but my friend is."

"Oh! You play in Daddy's band, don't you? I've seen you here before."

"That's right. Your Mummy and Daddy asked me if I wanted to go for a picnic with you today so I thought I'd better get here early in case you all went without me!" The twins leapt up shouting and cheering.

"Hooray, we're going on a picnic!" shouted Danielle.

"Where are we going Daddy?" asked Sophie.

"We're going to the New Forest to see if the chestnuts are ready." More shouting and yelling ensued.

"I don't suppose there's any hope of you two going back to bed for another hour?" asked Trish hopefully. "It's very early!"

"OH MUMMY!" they yelled together.

"OK, OK. You'd better get dressed then. When you're ready you can help me make the picnic."

The two of them scampered off like mad puppies. After a few seconds they could hear the twins arguing, and then Danielle came to the top of the stairs.

"Mummy! Sophie wants to take my teddy on the picnic."

"We aren't taking any teddies with us. They will just get lost or dirty."

"But Mum?"

"But nothing Danny! Get dressed!" They could hear her stomping back to her room. Another minute passed, then one of them let out a howl. Sophie came down the stairs in just her pyjama bottoms, tears pouring down her cheeks.

"Danny pinched me!" she howled, rubbing a tell-tale red mark on her arm.

"DANNY!" roared Trish, marching up the stairs with

Sophie. "Just one more thing and you stay behind!" She looked sternly at Sophie who was looking smug. "And that goes for you too! Now GET DRESSED!" Blissful silence followed for a few minutes, then two little girls in matching jeans and T-shirts came downstairs, and followed Mum into the kitchen, where they started arguing over the breakfast cereals. Ed looked at Mike.

"Is it always like this?" he asked.

"No. They're just showing off because you're here," he said cheerfully. "Usually they're much worse!"

That Saturday was a day that he would always remember with pleasure, a day of sunny skies and summer leaves turning gold; of children with auburn hair running through the dappled light under russet trees. Like a pair of spaniels kept indoors too long then set free, the girls ran like wild things in their natural element, laughing and shrieking through the trees with Mike crashing after them, striding out like some mythical ogre. Ed watched them with envy, wishing desperately that he had brought his camera with him. When they had all calmed down a little, Mike pointed out the bright coloured toadstools and the tall conical ant hills. The girls were clearly fascinated by any form of wildlife, and were soon scurrying off to find treasures of their own, eagerly showing everyone strange shaped leaves or cones. At one point, Trish pointed into the dense dark pine plantation on their left and to the twin's delight they found themselves being watched by a small herd of deer, who suddenly darted off, bounding and leaping through the trees.

Eventually they found a group of chestnut trees, heavy with the green, spiky nuts. There weren't many on the ground yet so Mike threw a branch up a few times to knock them down till Trish told him off. Quite a few fell to the ground, and though they weren't ready yet, they collected them anyway into a carrier bag brought specially for the job. The twins picked them up gingerly with their fingertips, squealing when they got prickled. When the bag was half full, they headed back to the car. Mike drove a large navy people carrier, which doubled up nicely for taking his musical equipment.

Trish and the girls had packed a proper hamper full of sandwiches and crisps and fruitcake. It looked like enough to feed an army! There was a huge open stretch of green grass next to the car park, nibbled short by the ponies, and several other families were already picnicking. A few yellow flowers still clung to the gorse bushes round the edge of the clearing, and their smell was warm and sweet. They found a quiet spot and Mike and Ed spread out two car rugs while Trish unpacked. There was a bottle of orange squash and a flask of coffee. They handed round plastic picnic plates and sat munching happily in the sun.

Despite the disastrous start to his day, Ed was feeling more carefree than he had for ages. He lay back on the rug when he had finished, and wondered if things would have been different for him and Lisa if they had had kids. For the first time in his life he could see that this was where it was at. He tried to remember days like this with his own family when he and Lara were children, but couldn't recall any.

Ed could hear Trish tidying away the picnic things, and the twins were getting bored and starting to argue again. Mike was lying on his front with his head on his hands. Ed sat up and offered to take the hamper back to the car. Mike threw him the keys and he headed back to the car park, returning with the bats and balls. Danny and Sophie's eyes lit up, and they ran round him with excitement. He started off a rather disorganised game of football, and after a while Mike came to join them. The few New Forest ponies grazing nearby shied away when the bright pink football came too close.

There was a lot of cheating going on, and Trish was cheering and booing from the sidelines. Then Sophie wanted to open the bat and ball game, and they devised a kind of home made rounders. The girls begged their Mum to join in, so Trish reluctantly got up from where she had been dozing in the sun, her early morning finally catching up with her. Ed was the first to be batted out, and walked back to the blanket in disgrace, followed swiftly and deliberately by Trish. Mike stayed out and played with the girls, trying in vain to inject some sense of sportsmanship into the game. When he returned, Trish and Ed were both flat out, one on each rug, fast asleep. He took the girls off for another short walk and a game of eye-spy and left the two sleepy heads in peace to catch up on their beauty sleep.

Chapter 9

That evening, Mike and Ed left early for the gig, so that Ed could get changed and collect his own car. They were playing at the Victoria Towers Hotel again, at an association dinner dance. For the first time ever, Ed had trouble concentrating on his music and made several mistakes. Mike pretended not to notice, and the audience certainly seemed happy with their performance, but Mike was worried and tried to insist that Ed slept over at their house that night. Ed politely but firmly refused, needing his own space for a while, and insisting that he was OK.

After the gig, and unusually for him, Ed went straight home. He felt uncomfortable about going for his usual kebab, feeling as though his every movement was being watched, and preferred instead to sit at home with a slice of toast and a mug of tea.

Next morning, Sunday, Ed was woken up by a ring on his doorbell. Each flatlet had its own bell, but as he very rarely got visitors, he was shocked by how loud his sounded. He hauled on his jeans and wrapped a shirt round him as he went down the stairs, praying it wasn't the police. In a way it was! Dave Walker was standing on the step, grinning his usual broad grin.

"Hello Mate! Hope I didn't wake you!"

"No problem. What can I do for you?" asked Ed cautiously.

"Can I come in? It's OK! It's not official."

"Course! Got time for a cuppa?"

"Thanks. They won't miss me for half an hour." Dave followed Ed through the hall and up the stairs, looking round in curiosity.

"Not a bad place this," he said.

"Yeah, right!" replied Ed.

"No seriously," continued Dave. "I've been called to nearly every rented block in Bournemouth at one time or another, but I've never been here."

"Well, most of the tenants are elderly and seem to have been here since the year dot!" replied Ed, filling the kettle. "It's fine most of the time, except for the lady downstairs who sometimes complains about the noise."

"That's a pain!" said Dave.

"Not really. This place suits me fine for now. They tell me she complains about everything, so if you do ever get called to a murder here, I'll bet you a tenner it's her!"

"Right!" laughed Dave. "I'll bare that in mind. Seriously though, I've come to see if you're alright, and to apologise. I never dreamt they would try to put you in the frame."

"That's OK. I never thought you had anything to do with it. I'm lucky that Trish knew what to do."

"Yes! She's a cracker! Mercier had a right cob on for the rest of the morning. I was quite relieved to be taken off the case. He's giving the other guys hell. I guess they're getting pressure from above. I ought to warn you, though, that he's probably still got his eye on you."

"Oh! Nice! Thanks for that!" said Ed passing him his tea.

They chatted for a while, till Dave made his excuses and went back to work. When he had gone, Ed felt even more depressed and went to run himself a hot, deep bath, and hide from the world.

Ed lay back and relaxed, up to his chin in warm bubbles. The weather looked as though it was going to be good. He wondered how he was going to spend his Sunday. This time it didn't feel like a treat, but instead the day seemed to loom interminably ahead of him. As it was Sunday, he guessed that Mike and Trish might invite him over for a roast dinner that evening. He felt that he ought to get back in touch with Sharon, but that might mean seeing Daz, and he wasn't looking forward to that meeting. He was also still puzzled about the white car. He really should go back to the hospital to see how Helen was doing, but the thought of it was depressing, and he knew that Dave would call him if there was any change. He waited till the water was luke warm, then reluctantly he got out of the bath and dried himself, returning to his room wearing just a towel.

While he was dressing, the news came on the radio. The murder of a teenage foreign language student was the headline. Apparently the seventeen year old girl had been walking back through Bournemouth towards the home of her host family at about midnight when the attack happened. Police were not yet releasing the name of the victim and were once again appealing for witnesses.

The newsreader went on to the next item and Ed realized that he was shivering, standing damp and naked in the middle of his room. Just to hear a friendly voice, he rang Sharon to ask if she had heard the news. She hadn't. She had only just woken up. Despite being Sunday, most of the shops would be open today. Ed invited her over to the flat for a coffee, and then into Bournemouth for lunch and some shopping.

"I'd love to. This time, give me your address and I'll get the bus over."

"Are you sure?"

"Yes. I've got to have a bath and do a couple of things before I can come out. Will elevenish be OK?" That gave Ed an hour and a half to tidy up and maybe get some biscuits in.

"That'll be great!" He gave her the address and said "See you then!" Once again she had sounded pleased and excited and Ed looked forward to seeing her. He pottered round, picking up clothes and straightening the bed. Then he dusted the obvious bits and pushed the sweeper around. He looked at his watch. Still an hour to go. He grabbed his jacket and headed for the Patel's shop.

Pearl was sweeping up, and beamed him a big toothy smile as he came in. She was wearing the big turquoise floral mumu, and festoons of silver today instead of gold.

"Ah Eddie! How are you today?"

"I'm fine. And what about you, you gorgeous creature!" Pearl giggled like a girl and rolled her eyes at him.

"I am still waiting for you to say you'll run away with me!"

"Soon, Pearl. Soon," he said soothingly. To his horror, Mr Patel appeared in the doorway of the stockroom.

"Edward!" he said. "I feel unable to compete with such unbridled passion. By all means take her away. Now this minute!"

"You know I would Mr P, but I am entertaining another young lady today. I only came in for a packet of biscuits. Got any custard creams?"

"Edward!" said Pearl. "You are shameless! Is it by any chance the lovely Sharon?"

"Yes Pearl, it is."

"And you think you will impress the young lady by showing her your custard creams?"

"Pearl! You have a one track mind! Anyway, I'm not trying to impress her. She's just a friend."

"Maybe to you, but I have seen the way she looks at you. Tell me, where are you two going?"

"I will tell you all about it tomorrow," promised Ed as he hastily paid for his biscuits before Pearl could give him the third degree.

As he left the shop, he saw a familiar figure in the distance, walking along the littered pavement towards him. It was Daz! He walked straight up to Ed with his eyes blazing, so close that their faces were barely inches apart. Ed could feel the spittle on his cheek as he spoke.

"I've been looking for you, you bastard!" he hissed "Stay

away from my mother or else!" Ed was stunned and, for a second, he didn't know what to say. Daz continued.

"Have you got that?"

"What the hell are you on about?" asked Ed finally.

"Just bugger off! OK? We don't need no posh git hanging around. Leave us alone or else."

"Or else what?" asked Ed, getting annoyed now. The thought of Daz threatening him was somehow laughable. "What are you gonna do?"

"You really don't want to find that out!" Ed looked him straight in the eye, and suddenly it wasn't laughable any more. It wasn't even Daz any more. There was something cold and chilling in his eyes. "Screw with my Mother and you screw with me! It's your choice." Even his voice had changed. Ed just stared back at him hoping he would drop his gaze first, but he didn't. They stood there in the street, eye to eye, till Ed could stand it no longer. He suddenly laughed in Daz's face and said,

"Grow up!" before turning smartly on his heel and walking away. As he left, he heard Daz call out after him,

"Don't say I didn't warn you!"

Ed walked back towards the flat, deep in thought. Had that really been a chance meeting, or had Daz been looking for him. He hoped that Daz didn't know his address, and he hung around for a bit, just to make sure he wasn't followed. Did Daz know that Ed was seeing Sharon today? Probably not. They had only just arranged it. He decided not to tell her about the meeting. After all, Daz was just a jealous, mixed up kid.

Sharon turned up at ten to eleven and they sat on the sofa together, chiefly as there was nothing else to sit on. She looked really nice today and was wearing a long flowing skirt with a ruffled blouse and cropped suede jacket. They soon got chatting over coffee, and Sharon asked after Helen.

"I haven't seen her for a couple of days, and I really ought to, but I just can't face it," he said.

"Would you go if I came with you?"

"I couldn't put you through that! It really is so depressing."

"But I'd like to. If it would help, that is."

"Well. I suppose it would make it easier," he said, coming round to the idea. "It's her parents! They just sit in silence, and I don't know what to say. They want to be told it's going to be alright, and I can't do that."

"Do you really need to go at all?" she asked gently.

"Yes, I do."

"Well, lets get it over and done with first. Then we can go shopping with a clear conscience!" she declared. Ed smiled at her.

"You really are good for me, you know!" he said.

"I know!" she replied with feeling.

For the first time, there was no-one in the ward with Helen. Two metal chairs were pulled up to the bed, and on the back of one of them hung a cardigan. Ed and Sharon looked down on Helen's lifeless face and Ed took hold of her frail hand.

"Hello again Helen. I've brought my friend Sharon to see you."

"Can she hear us?" whispered Sharon.

"I've no idea. Probably not!" He held on tightly to her hand and continued to talk in a quiet, steady voice. "Everyone is waiting for you to get better; your Mum, Dad, me and Sharon. Your Aunt Lou has been in, and a very handsome policeman called Dave. You'll want to wake up and see him. All the girls like Dave." He was running out of things to say. He turned to look at Sharon, and was touched to see tears welling up in her eyes. He felt himself filling up too, and turned his attention back towards the figure in the bed.

A sound behind them made Ed turn, and a young nurse entered. Ed called her over.

"How is she?"

"Are you family?"

"No. I'm the man who found her."

"Ah! You must be Edward. Mrs Parrott told me you'd been visiting."

"Is it OK for us to be here?" asked Sharon.

"Yes, I don't see why not. She is still a very sick girl I'm afraid. She has suffered a skull fracture and three broken ribs, as well as severe bruising. She should be regaining consciousness any time now."

"Can she hear us?" asked Ed.

"It's quite possible. I'd say that it can't do any harm to talk to her, and it might easily be doing some good. Her parents should be back soon. They've just popped down for a paper."

"Thank you," said Ed. The nurse smiled and left the room. Ed took Helen's hand again, and Sharon sat beside him.

"Poor little thing. She looks so helpless."

"Her Aunt told me she's a right little tearaway."

"No-one deserves this," she said. "I hope when they catch this,... this animal, they string him up by the balls. There's no punishment bad enough for a man who could do this to a young girl. None!" Ed could see she was genuinely upset, and decided it was time to go. He had promised her a nice day, and this wasn't really her problem. Still holding Helen's hand, Ed said goodbye.

"We've got to go now, but we'll be back soon." He lifted her little hand and kissed it lightly. "Goodbye." Suddenly he felt her squeeze his hand.

"Did you see that? Helen? Helen?" He turned to Sharon. "Get the nurse!"

She ran out and returned seconds later with the same nurse, who took Helen's hand from Ed.

"Helen?" she called. "Helen? Time to wake up now. Open your eyes Helen." Ed stepped back and let the nurse do her job. She turned to Ed.

"What exactly happened?"

"She squeezed my hand when I said goodbye."

"How many times?"

"Only once but it was quite firm."

"There's nothing now. Did you do anything else?"

"No! Yes! I lifted it."

"It might just be an involuntary spasm. Or she might be coming back to us."

Just then Mr and Mrs Parrott returned. Mary Parrott saw the group around the bed and gave a little scream. The group parted as Mary rushed forwards, with the nurse explaining calmly what was happening. Dennis started to sob, and Mary wept openly while holding her daughter's hand and begging her to come back. Ed and Sharon crept away leaving them to it.

"Oh God! I hope I haven't raised their hopes for nothing!" said Ed.

"They needed some little crumb of comfort," she said, squeezing his arm. "Do you really think she heard you?"

"I can't be sure, but I think so!"

Ed parked on the cliff top, just past the Russel Cotes museum, a beautiful mansion overlooking the sea with balconies and turrets and magnificent stained glass. The owners had filled their home with treasures from their travels around the world, before leaving it to the people of the town. Now it was open to the public, and was kept in beautiful condition by the local council and a willing band of volunteers. Ed and Sharon peered in as they passed the front door.

"Have you ever been in?" asked Ed.

"No, but I keep meaning to," replied Sharon. "It looks fascinating."

"We'll have to pop in for afternoon tea!"

"Oh, how very civilised." It was such a lovely day and Ed kept getting the urge to hold her hand. A smile crossed his face as he had a sudden vision of Daz, leaping out from behind a bush at them, crazed and scary, so he left Sharon's hand where it was.

"What are you smiling at?" she asked.

"Oh nothing!" he said. "What exactly are you shopping for?" Neither of them had mentioned Helen since they had left the hospital, and it was hard to know what else to talk about.

"Shall I write you a list?"

"Better not!" he said "Just lead on. I'm only here to carry the bags!"

Two and a half hours later Sharon had bought a pair of cropped jeans, two T-shirts and a blouse. It had been hard work, persuading her to try things on, and even harder getting her to let him see. Some things hadn't suited her at all, and Ed had been honest. Most of the time she agreed with him anyway, and came to trust his opinion. He had started by suggesting the sort of clothes which had looked good on Lisa; this being his only real point of reference. He soon came to realize that their style was completely different. To be honest, Lisa had a smashing figure, and had looked good in almost anything. Sharon was shorter and curvy, and certain clothes just made her look dumpy. However, she had smashing boobs, and well cut clothes made her look quite sexy and voluptuous in a way that Lisa's 'clothes horse' figure never had. He found he was a little ashamed to be mentally comparing the two, but at least he was pretty well schooled in saying all the right things!

They stopped for lunch in a coffee bar which made their own pasties and Danish pastries. They both ordered the cheese and onion quiche with salad, and a cappuccino each. Ed put the shopping bags down on an empty seat at their table and sugared his coffee. Sharon was looking very pleased with herself.

"I haven't bought myself this many new clothes in ages," she said. "I'll have to bring you shopping with me every time. You're a good influence!"

"No! No!" cried Ed. "Spare me!"

"Oh come on! I haven't been that bad. Have I?"

"No. Actually I like everything you've bought. It was an

experience!"

"Tell you what!" she said. "After lunch I'll find some things for you to try on."

"But I don't need any new clothes!"

"Try some things on anyway."

"What for?"

"Because it's the closest I'm ever likely to come to getting your kit off!" Ed was slightly shocked, and found himself blushing.

"Eat your lunch, you hussy!"

They finished off the quiche, which was delicious, and Ed ordered some more coffee. Neither could manage a dessert, despite the Danish pastries looking so tempting. "How's Daz?" asked Ed innocently.

"Oh, a pain in the arse as usual. He won't tell me where he's been or why. He just sits in his bedroom with the door locked."

"Hasn't he told you anything?"

"He did say that someone was after him for money, but that was weeks ago. God knows what he's been up to this time. I phoned the petrol station yesterday, but they won't give him his job back."

"That's a shame. I expect he could use the money."

"We both could!"

"It must have been hard for you when his Dad died." Sharon looked amazed.

"I don't know where you got that from! Unfortunately my ex husband is alive and well and living with some little tart in Croydon. Who told you he was dead?" Ed had trouble concealing his anger. Was everything Daz told him a pack of lies?

He looked up at Sharon and smiled brightly.

"I'm sorry. I must have got the wrong end of the stick." Just wait till he got his hands on him! He quickly changed the subject. "By the way. Thanks for coming with me to the hospital."

"That's OK. I only hope she recovers soon. How often do you visit her?"

"The last time was Friday evening. In fact I nearly came round to see you after, but I didn't think Daz would appreciate the visit."

"What time was that?" she asked.

"About ten I think. Why?"

"I wish you had. Me and Daz were having a right shouting match, and then he stormed out. He didn't come back till yesterday. He has gone really weird lately. I just don't know what to do with him."

"Does he know that you're seeing me today."

"No," she replied. "I couldn't face telling him."

"Mm. Probably best not!" Slowly, piece by piece, things were coming together in Ed's mind. Dark suspicions started forming, and he drained his coffee cup and tried to push them aside.

"What's up?" asked Sharon.

"Oh nothing much. Did you say that Daz was out on Friday night?"

"Yes. All night! He left in a real temper because I wouldn't lend him a tenner. I'd never have got it back."

"About what time was that?" asked Ed.

"Must have been around nine. Why?"

"No reason."

Friday night was the night when a young foreign student was murdered in Bournemouth town centre. Ed was sure his suspicions were wrong. Nevertheless, it wouldn't hurt to find out where Daz had been during the two previous attacks.

Chapter 10

For the next few days, the murder hunt was followed keenly by the press. Television cameras were taken to the scene, and the girl's parents had come over to England, and were shown weeping openly on TV. Her name was Claudia De Sousa, and she was a Spanish student, staying with a host family in Bournemouth to learn English. Her photo had been splashed over the local and national papers, and on the telly, so that her face was becoming familiar. The picture showed a girl with dark curly hair and brown eyes, laughing at the camera with all the carefree attitude of her age. It was almost cruel in the way that she smiled straight at you, so pretty and so happy, when you knew that her young life had just been snuffed out by one sick individual.

Ed had fully been expecting Mercier to get back in contact, and when he didn't, the suspense became too much and Ed phoned Dave Walker. Dave wasn't answering his mobile so Ed left a message on his voice mail.

"Hi Mate; Ed here! Just need to know what's going on. Is Mercier still on my case? Hope you're OK. We must catch up over a pint soon. Call me when you get a moment. Bye!"

It was the next day when Dave called back.

"Sorry mate. They've put me back on the case, and I've been working all the hours they can give me. I need the overtime!"

"That's OK. Any news?"

"Well, we've had a couple of leads but nothing concrete yet. The trouble is with random attacks, there is very little to go on until he makes a mistake. We've got a trainer print, but it's a common make, and hundreds of people walk their dogs down there so it could be anyone's."

"Anything else?"

"Sorry Ed. I really can't tell you any more. You know how it is."

"Fair enough."

"I've been hanging around the hospital a lot, waiting for Helen to regain consciousness. She's the only one who can tell us anything."

"Any news there?"

"Well, she's moved her head and her hand a couple of times, but nothing more yet. We've got someone down there twenty four hours now, but the ward sister is watching over her like a guard dog."

"That's a point!" said Ed. "Might she be in danger, if the attacker thinks she could identify him?"

"It's a possibility. In fact, it might be as well for you to stay away from the hospital for the next couple of days. They aren't letting in anyone except family at the moment anyway."

"OK. Point taken."

"And thanks for the offer of a pint. We've got a lot of catching up to do! Do you mind if we take a reign-check though, till this investigation's over."

"No! You can't be seen out boozing with one of the suspects!"

"Sorry but you've hit the nail on the head! This job can be a real bastard with your mates. I really want to know what you've been up to though."

"Yes, and you too. I'd better let you go."

"OK, see you."

"Bye!"

Ed felt as though his life had been put on ice. He worked at the shop most days, and Mike or Trish had phoned nearly every day for a chat, but he preferred to spend most of his free time at home, working alone on the guitar. He had been putting together new material for his act from his old CD's and songs recorded from the radio, and was now working out the cords and lyrics. He also practised some of the stuff he had written himself, but his imagination seemed to have dried up for the time being, and he found himself unable to write anything new.

Sharon had phoned a couple of times, once to thank him, and once to ask him out for a drink. He had refused, firmly but politely, and she had taken the hint and not called again. It was strange how he found himself starting to miss her, but while he had suspicions in his head about Daz, he couldn't face her and pretend that everything was alright. That would be like betraying her trust, so he decided that it was all too complicated and that he should just stay away.

Ed was surprised when Dave phoned again that day.

"Hi Ed. I'm at the hospital."

"Oh! How's Helen?"

"The same I'm afraid. Listen," he said. "I've got a message for you. It's from Mary Parrot's sister, Lou. I didn't realise you two were friends." Ed laughed.

"OK, OK. I know you're going to think I'm crazy but she's actually a psychic or something. She reckons she can help catch the killer."

"Great! Hey, I can really see Mercier going for that! You're not serious are you?"

"To be honest Dave," said Ed, "I had a talk with her, and she really put the shits up me. She knew all sorts of stuff." Dave remained silent. "Look, I've never believed in any of that but now,… I'm not so sure."

"Whatever you think mate, but mind you don't stick your neck out. You know what I mean. Mercier would love to chop it off!"

"OK! Received and understood!" said Ed. "What's the message?"

"She wants to meet you in reception this afternoon. Shall I give her a time?"

"Tell her I'll be there at three o'clock?"

"Will do. See you later!"

"Thanks Dave. Bye."

"Bye."

When Ed arrived at the hospital, Lou was already sitting at a table in the café area of the reception with a cup of tea. Ed bought himself a coffee and went to join her. When she saw him she stood up and shook his hand like a man.

"Thank you for coming Edward."

"That's all right Lou. Nice to see you again. What can I do for you?"

"I'll get right to the point!" she said sitting down. "I know it's a cheek, but would you mind taking me to the spot where that poor girl was killed. You see I don't drive, and what on earth would I tell the taxi driver?"

"I see your point," said Ed. "Of course I will, if that's what you want. Shall we go now?"

"Oh Edward. You are a dear! I knew you'd understand."

He parked at the far end of Bourneside park as it was a residential area with easier parking. They walked together to the top of the path and peered down it. The strip of tarmac was only about a metre wide and about a hundred metres long. As they walked along, it curved gently so that only a short section in the middle was invisible from the road at either end. Both sides of the path were a mixture of grass, trees and clumps of bushes, with older style street lamps dotted at regular intervals, plus a couple of concrete benches and a dog bin.

The path had been re-opened but there was still crime-scene tape strung in the bushes, and a large patch of well trodden grass to mark where the murder had taken place. Ed and Lou found themselves totally alone as they approached. Ed felt a little sickened and sat heavily on one of the concrete benches leaving Lou to do her stuff. He watched as she poked around a bit, then intermittently stopped and closed her eyes for a few moments, before continuing again. Eventually, she came and sat next to him. Ed spoke first.

"You know that I'm a suspect, don't you?"

"Yes. I rather thought you might be."

"You don't mind being here alone with me then?" asked Ed. She turned her head and smiled at him.

"No, Ed. I'm quite sure that I'm perfectly safe."

"How?"

"Because he only goes for young, pretty ones!" She got up again and started pacing around like a restless cat. Then she stopped in the middle of the path with her eyes shut, till a man with a dog grunted as he tried to get by.

"Oh, I am sorry!" said Lou, embarrassed. She sat down again. Ed stayed silent, convinced that this was just a waste of time. Why was he sat on a bench in the middle of nowhere humouring this nutty old woman?

"Was it a penknife?" asked Lou suddenly.

"What?" replied Ed.

"The weapon! Was it a penknife?"

"I don't know. Is it important?"

"It might be. Can you find out?"

"I think so," said Ed. He got out his mobile phone and dialled up Dave's number.

Dave answered immediately.

"What is it Ed? I'm driving."

"I need to know if the murder weapon was a penknife?"

"What?"

"Was it a penknife?" The line went silent for a few seconds and then Dave said,

"Where are you?"

"Bourneside Park, at the scene."

Dave sounded tense. "Stay there! I'll be five minutes!" and rang off. He was there in just under ten, striding towards them with his long mack flapping behind him. His faced looked anxious and strained as he nodded a greeting to Lou and sat heavily next to Ed.

"Why did you ask me about the penknife?" he asked. Ed shrugged and looked at Lou.

"I was right then," she said.

"No-one is supposed to know about that," continued Dave. "I need to know how you do. And don't give me that psychic rubbish either!" Ed stood up so that they could talk without him in the middle. He turned to face them, wondering how he had let himself be talked into this situation so easily. For Christ's sake, Dave had even tried to warn him against getting involved.

"I can only tell you if you are willing to listen, and try to understand," said Lou stubbornly.

"Try me," said Dave patiently.

"I see things; flashes. I pick up vibrations, thoughts even! Are you with me so far?"

"I'm trying," said Dave. "What did you see?"

"I think it must be what that girl saw, Claudia. It was a fist, holding one of those fancy penknives with all the bits on; Swiss army, I think they call them."

"Go on," said Dave

"It was dark red plastic with a dull sort of silver blade, and a shiny symbol of some kind on the side. I couldn't quite make it out."

"Anything else?"

"No. Well, maybe."

Lou rummaged through her bag and took out the drawing of the square surrounding the circle she had made at the hospital. "I saw this at the scene of the attack on Helen, and also through Helen herself when I was holding her hand. Does it mean anything to you?"

Dave studied the picture and shook his head. "No. Can I keep it?"

"Yes, if you like," replied Lou. Dave put the paper in his pocket and got up.

"Look," he said. "I'll have to think carefully before I decide what to do. Thank you for your help, Mrs Dodds. Ed? Could I have a word?"

Dave and Ed walked off along the path together leaving Lou alone on the bench for a minute. Dave stopped when they were out of hearing and turned to face Ed.

"Do you realize what's happening here?"

"I think so, but tell me anyway," replied Ed.

"We are withholding the information that the attack was carried out with a large penknife. Then lo and behold, you phone up and tell me what the murder weapon was. This is the break we have been waiting for. You are now our number one suspect. No-one is going to believe that bunkum about a bloody psychic seeing it in a vision."

"What are you going to do?" asked Ed.

"You tell me! If I tell them, you'll be locked up as quick as a flash, and don't think your red headed little friend can help you this time. You have proven knowledge of the crime. If I don't tell them, and it ever comes out, I am an officer withholding evidence. I'll lose my job, and I've worked bloody hard to get where I am."

"What about if Lou comes to the station and volunteers the information over the desk?" asked Ed hopefully. "You know the attacker is a man so you are hardly going to arrest her!"

"Let me think about it. You've put me in one hell of a position."

"I'm sorry. Tell me something though, Dave. Do you honestly think I had anything to do with it?"

"No, Ed. I don't think you did. But if you didn't, then you're asking me to believe in spirits and mediums, and I don't buy that either!" With that he turned and stalked back up the path, his coat flapping behind him in the breeze. Ed watched him departing with a feeling of regret. Here endeth another friendship!

He returned to Lou with a heavy heart.

"I don't think your friend is very pleased with us," she said.

"Don't worry Lou. I've just put him on the spot, that's all."

"I'm sorry Ed. You'd better take me home if you don't mind, before I get you into any more trouble."

Ed drove her back to her modest little bungalow, a couple of miles away. She didn't get out of the car immediately, but seemed to be summing up the courage to speak.

"If I ask you something, will you give me a straight answer?"

"If I can," replied Ed.

"Do you know who it is?" Ed stared straight through the windscreen.

"No," he replied truthfully.

"But you think you know, don't you?" Ed remained silent.

"If you know something Ed, you must tell. What about Dave walker? He seems a good sort." Ed finally answered her.

"I have a vague suspicion, that's all. It's very complicated and I've no proof at all. It involves someone I care about, you see."

"It's your decision," said Lou. "Just don't put yourself in any danger. If you find that proof, you owe it to a lot of people to tell." Ed looked at her.

"If I find out anything for sure," he said solemnly "I promise I will."

Ed drove home deep in thought. He pulled up in a space on the East Cliff, got out of the car and leant his elbows on the top of the fence, staring out to sea. The sun was still shining but a sharp little wind was cutting straight through his shirt, making him shiver. He didn't care. All was not well with Ed's world. He had come to Bournemouth to escape the turmoil of a broken marriage, which seemed small fry when compared to being chucked headlong into the middle of a murder investigation. He had fallen out with Dave, Sharon, Daz, his wife, and last but not least his own family. The unfairness of it all was that he didn't really ask for any of it. He was a peace loving soul, who had never knowingly hurt anyone. How had he got himself into this mess? Suddenly the answer to his questions appeared as if by magic. A small figure was walking towards him along the cliff top, duffel coat flapping and sticky up hair ruffling in the wind.

"Daz!" shouted Ed at the top of his voice. Daz stopped, recognising Ed and unsure what to do. "Daz!" Suddenly he turned and ran away. Ed was in no mood to mess about, and he gave chase. Daz ran along the pavement and turned swiftly down the path that zig zagged down the cliff towards the beach. He was fast and light, and Ed lost sight of him round the sharp twists in the path. When Ed burst out onto the promenade, it took a few seconds to spot which way Daz had gone. He suddenly saw him a good distance away, running past stacks of deckchairs on the prom. Ed continued to run, angry now. The little bastard was brave enough the last time he saw him. What was he afraid of now? Daz was fit from years of having to walk everywhere, and kept on going like a greyhound, but Ed was used to running, and slowly but surely started to gain on him. They kept on and on till Ed's lungs were burning and his legs started to feel like lead, but Daz kept on going. The chase was turning into some sort of personal challenge. Eventually Ed was almost close enough to reach out and touch him, and he could hear Daz's breaths coming in great sobs. Daz looked over his shoulder and in desperation, hurled himself down the short, rocky slope onto the sand.

Running on sand is a killer, and in the last stages of exhaustion, damn near impossible. Fiery pain took hold of Ed's calf muscles as he ploughed through the soft surface towards his quarry, feeling for the first time a grudging respect for Daz's endurance. Daz was floundering, and headed for the firmer sand at the water's edge, with Ed only inches behind. Daz hit the firm sand first, and with a new burst of speed, put another couple of metres between them. Ed knew he had nothing left, and took a flying jump at Daz's departing back, knocking him face down into the shallow water.

A small wave washed over Daz's face and he choked and spluttered. His body was craving for oxygen and all he got was a lungful of salt water and sand. Ed was lying across the top of him, too exhausted to move. As Daz coughed, Ed grabbed a handful of the hair on the back of his head and pulled his face clear of the water. Then he rolled off him and pulled Daz over so they were lying on their backs in the shallows, gasping and choking, too shattered to speak. They lay there side by side like two stranded fish for a good few minutes, till the life started returning to Ed's Body. Finally, as his breathing became easier, he sat up and said,

"Right you little shit! I need some answers." Daz struggled to a sitting position and Ed saw big fat tears rolling down his cheeks. He grabbed the top of Daz's arm and half dragged him up the beach, where he sat on the stone steps, pulling the sobbing, gasping boy down beside him.

"What's going on with you, Daz? I don't get it."

"You wouldn't understand," replied Daz.

"Well you'd better make me understand, because we're not going anywhere till I do!"

"OK. What do you want to know?"

"Well for a start, you can tell me why you want everyone to think your Mum's some kind of drug crazed alcoholic." Daz didn't answer so Ed continued in disgust. "And why did you tell me that your Dad's dead?"

"He might as well be!" shouted Daz.

"That's not the point! I've never met your Dad so maybe he deserved it, but you've got a great Mum," said Ed. "She really cares about you."

"How was I to know that you knew her?" asked Daz. Ed was even more disgusted with him.

"For God's sake Daz! Why?"

"Because I tell lies, OK?" he sobbed. "I don't know why I do it. They just come out."

"But that's your Mum!"

"I know, and I feel bad. I just want to be different, interesting. Nobody wants to listen to what I have to say, so I make stuff up." Ed gave up and changed the subject.

"Tell me where you were on that Thursday night, when you asked me to look out for you," said Ed. "And why did you disappear for so long after."

"I was there, and you didn't show up," said Daz angrily. "I got worked over because of you!" He glared accusingly at Ed.

"I was there. I was just a couple of minutes late, that's all," replied Ed. "Did you go into the graveyard? Did you call out my name?" Daz nodded miserably. So he hadn't been hearing things after all. Ed tried another tack.

"Who owns the white Mondeo?" This time, Daz looked at him with wide eyes. Ed saw his fear and pushed home his advantage. "Just tell me what the bloody hell's going on or I'll go to the police."

"If I tell you," asked Daz, "you must promise you won't tell. They'll kill me if you do." Ed quickly summed up his options and nodded. He'd try not to, but honour didn't mean much to Daz. Personally at this moment, Ed would love to see Daz locked up!

"You can trust me," he said, "but I must have the whole story."

"The car belongs to Les."

"Who's Les?" asked Ed.

"He's Mum's ex-boyfriend. He's supplies drugs to the dealers."

"Go on!"

"He uses the petrol station where I work as a drop off."

"I see," said Ed. "Tell me how it works."

"I meet him at night in the top car park, and he gives me the stuff in sealed packets. I take it to work and he texts my mobile when someone is coming in to collect. Then I go in the toilet and hide it in the top of the towel dispenser. Someone comes in to buy petrol, and uses the loo. I go in after and collect the cash from the same place, usually rolled up in a fag packet. I take it back to Les in the car park and he pays me and gives me the next lot." Ed thought about this for a second, then asked,

"Why all the subterfuge in the toilet. Why not just hand it over?"

"Because Les says that known dealers are watched all the time, and no-one's going to suspect a guy buying petrol. Besides, there's a CCTV camera trained on the counter." Ed thought about it for a moment. It was a perfect set-up. If the police were looking for a meeting, there wouldn't be one.

"So why is this Les after you?"

"Because I lost a packet."

"How?"

"There's a hole in my duffel coat lining. Mum's been on at me about it for ages. It must have fallen through!"

"No wonder they were after you. They must have thought you were ripping them off," said Ed. "What was in it?"

"Nearly eight hundred quid," replied Daz. Ed whistled.

"So you wanted me to be there when you broke the bad news." Daz nodded. "So what happened next?"

"There were two of them in the car. I told Les what happened, and he told his mate to get me. I ran like hell down the path, but he caught me near the church. Les brought the car round to the gate and they shoved me in and brought me down here. They were going to beat me up, but I bit the guy holding me and got away. I slept in the railway station that night and got a train to Southampton first thing in the morning."

"Then what?"

"I met some guys with a squat and stayed there for a bit. It was horrible and smelly and they tried to steal my things. I couldn't come home though. Les would kill me!"

"So what's your Mum doing with a scum-bag like Les?"

"He's not a scum-bag, not when you meet him. He's smart and flashy, and women seem to like that. He treated her real nice too. I think he really liked her. He wanted to move in with us but Mum wouldn't let him. I swear she never knew about the drugs."

Ed sat and took it all in. At last things were beginning to add up and make sense. No wonder Daz was so angry when he thought that his Mum was seeing Ed. He remembered Sharon complaining about his mood swings, and the crazy way he had confronted Ed himself.

"Show me your arms!" said Ed. Daz looked defensive and put his arms behind his back. Ed spoke again. "Trust me. I just need to know." Daz shrugged and pulled up his left sleeve. The last few pieces of the puzzle fell into place. Ed had never actually seen the arm of an addict before except on the telly, and it was a shock. The veins were a mottled mess of stab marks and bruising. Well that explained the mood swings, and probably the lying too. He couldn't imagine what drove a person to inflict that much damage on themselves.

"Did Les pay you in drugs as well as cash?" Daz nodded again. It was easy to see how a gullible kid like Daz had been groomed as a carrier, and how Les had used this fragile little family as a cover for his evil business. Les was just a parasite, and he vowed to get even if it was the last thing he did……..

"Can I ask you something?" asked Daz.
"Sure!" said Ed.
"What are you doing with my Mum?" Ed nearly laughed out loud, but he could see that it was a valid question.
"I only met your Mum when I came looking for you. She was worried about you and, for my sins, so was I, so I agreed to help her find you."
"But how did you know where she lived?"
"Simon showed me."
"Oh!" said Daz. "So are you two seeing each other?"
"I'm not sleeping with her, if that's what you want to know. We really are just friends and I'm afraid you'll have to take my word for it." Daz blushed furiously.

"But I thought,…." said Daz, lamely.

"Yes, I know you did, but no offence, she really isn't my type, and I don't suppose I'm hers either," said Ed. "Listen Daz. Don't wish for bad parents, not even in pretend. Some people don't get a choice. Besides, you're all she's got."

"I thought she had you," said Daz. "I didn't think she needed me any more."

"Well you're wrong. From where I'm standing, I'd say you need each other. Just try being friends for a change. You might find you enjoy it!"

Chapter 11

Dave sat at his desk and stared moodily at his pencil. He was trying to balance it on the flat end so that it stood up straight like a Cleopatra's needle. As a pastime it was a frustrating choice. Ed's drawing sat on the desk in front of him. He had stared at it from all angles, trying to make sense of it. Then he had screwed it up in frustration and thrown it in the bin, then retrieved it again and smoothed it out as best he could. The problem of the penknife kept niggling him too, and he knew that if Ed hadn't been a mate, he would have told Mercier. You see, there was the question; was Ed a mate? No, he was an old school friend, but if you really thought about it, Dave didn't have any real mates left. Sarah had seen to that.

Dave had been married to Sarah for six years, and they had a boy and a girl, Ben aged five and Alice aged three. Right now they were going through a nasty divorce with a full blown custody row thrown in for good measure. It was probably Dave's fault. He had devoted all his energy to his career, and had got himself caught doing extra curriculum activities with a WPC. Now he was living with his parents in their cramped semi in Verwood. Since having kids, Sarah had begrudged him any time to himself so that his social life was now practically non existent. Sarah, in contrast, seemed to have gathered a whole army of 'coffee morning' mums around her, who were only too eager to hear what a bastard Dave Walker was. Egged on by her gang, she was now fleecing him for every penny he earned, and employing any tactic at her disposal to make his life a misery. To call Sarah bitter was the understatement of the century.

Meeting Ed again couldn't have come at a better time. Ed was obviously going through some sort of marital turmoil of his own, and he thought that it might be good to have someone to chew it all over with. Ed and Dave had been good mates since their first year in junior school. As kids they had spent many long summer days cycling together for miles, and it was Ed who had first taught him to fish. Dave had always looked up to Ed. His parents lived in a nice big house and had a posh car each. As teenagers they had spent many happy hours in Ed's bedroom listening to the latest music on his hi fi system. Dave's own upbringing had been far more modest. If he wanted to listen to music at home he had had to tune in his mother's radio in the kitchen.

Dave's pencil clattered to the desk for the twentieth time as his desk phone rang. He answered the phone with one hand while he dropped the pencil back into the desk tidy with the other. Then he hung up, grabbed his coat, and headed back to the hospital. Mercier had specifically asked for Dave to be there when she woke up. He would decide what to do about Ed later.

Ed took Daz, dripping and shivering, back to his flat where he made him a coffee and found him some dry clothes to change into, putting his wet things into a carrier. Daz's whinging and self pity was getting on Ed's nerves, and he reflected that if it hadn't been for Sharon, he could cheerfully have left the lying little sod to drown in the sea. He looked at the pathetic excuse sitting on his sofa, and thought for the umpteenth time that only a mother could love it! Would Daz ever become a man or was Sharon saddled with a waster for the rest of her life? Still, it wasn't his problem. He'd done his best, and now he had to leave them in peace to get on with their lives. He had a last, final stab at talking some sense into Daz.

"Daz? Do me a favour."

"What?"

"Go easy on your Mum, will you? I know you see her just as a Mum, but try to see things from her point of view a bit more."

"What do you mean?"

"Your Mum is just a nice young woman who's had a tough time, trying hard to keep a home together for a son who really doesn't appreciate her. You're old enough to take some responsibility for her too. She needs someone to turn to sometimes, we all do."

"What use am I going to be to anyone? Look at me!" He had a point, but at least he was listening. Ed kept trying.

"Does she know about your drug habit?" Daz shrugged.

"S'pose so," he said moodily. "She's probably guessed."

"She'd rather hear it from you, you know. And your gonna need all her help if you want to kick it," said Ed. "Talk to her! I know she'll understand."

"OK. I'll talk to her, but you'll keep quiet about the other thing, won't you?"

"I've already promised I won't tell her, but what are you going to do about Les. I don't like the thought of him hanging around."

"I'll sort it. Honest!" said Daz. Ed wondered if he knew what the word meant.

Ed had to leave it at that and let go. After all, Les's little scam with Daz was over and Daz hadn't been caught, so there was nothing to be gained by turning him in. The money Daz had lost was probably small change to a supplier like Les. He would be a fool to jeopardise his operation over one dozy kid and Ed didn't think for one moment that Les was a fool. He offered Daz a lift home but Daz said he had some thinking to do, and he could think best while he was walking, so Ed showed him out.

Dave noticed the change as soon as he entered the ward. Helen Parrott was sitting up in bed, chatting to her Mum and

Dad. Mary Parrott's face was a happy, blotchy mess. Dennis on the other hand sat quietly and contentedly at the foot of the bed. As usual he had very little to say but the look of desperation had gone from his eyes, replaced by the relief of a proud parent. Dave felt almost ashamed to intrude on their happiness, but as soon as Mary saw him, she dragged him into the scenario as though he were an old friend.

"She's back!" she told him simply. "Look!"

Dave grinned shyly at the pretty blonde with the bandaged head sitting before him. It was hard to believe this was the same girl he had seen being dragged, broken and bleeding, from the base of that tree only the week before. Helen smiled back. It was the first time Dave had seen her with her eyes open, and they were a startling combination of pale and dark blue. Despite the bruises and the bandages, she was a cracker.

Lou wasn't kidding when she said that Helen was a minx. Not only that but she was an accomplished tease and a flirt too. Although she had been awake for little over a hour, she had already managed to scrounge some make-up from one of the nurses plus some concealer for her bruises. Helen could vaguely recall someone telling her about a handsome policeman called Dave, but wasn't sure when. Wow! Perhaps being stuck in here a few more days wouldn't be so bad after all.

"Have you come to question me?" she asked boldly.

"Only when you feel up to it," he replied. "How are you feeling?"

"Not too bad," she said, but suddenly gave a big yawn. The nurse who was just looking in spotted Dave and nodded him over.

"You're not going to question her now are you?" she asked. "She needs some rest."

"No," said Dave. "It can wait a while. How is she?"

"Remarkable really," replied the nurse. "She opened her eyes and started chatting almost immediately. To be honest we were giving up hope of her making a full recovery. This is just fantastic!" Dave looked at her with admiration. She really cared.

"It's obviously important that we speak to her as soon as possible," he said. "This nutter is still on the loose."

"Of course. Can you come back after six? I'll try to make sure she's ready for you then."

"Thank you," said Dave.

"No problem," she replied. "Now I must get on!"

Dave went to say goodbye to Helen. She looked most disappointed.

"You will come back, won't you? We can talk now if you want!"

"I can't," said Dave. "That nurse would have my guts for garters!"

"Oh, that's Janice. You don't have to worry about her."

"But I do have to worry about you, and you need some rest! I'll be back this evening, OK?"

"OK," she said sulkily. "What time?"

"About sixish."

"It's a date then!" she said.

"Yep!" replied Dave with a smile. "It's a date!"

Dave went straight back to the station to find WPC Angela Smith. It was Angela who he'd had the fling with, but that was over months ago and the two of them had managed to maintain a reasonable working relationship. The affair had been the subject of office speculation and gossip for a while, but both the affair and the gossip had died a natural death. They decided that they didn't need the pressures of a work based relationship, but it had made Dave face up to the flaws in his own marriage.

When Sarah discovered his text messages, it was almost a relief that their problems would now be out in the open. It was also a relief that Dave didn't have to confront Sarah with the painful truth, for beyond anything else, he didn't want to hurt her. How could he tell her that he wanted out, that he no longer found her attractive. She had piled on the pounds, then the stones, and when he had tactfully broached the subject she had flown into a fury and blamed childbirth. She was always complaining that he didn't earn enough money and that he should be climbing the promotional ladder faster for the sake of her and the kids. Also that he didn't appreciate how hard she worked and that he should help round the house more.

Sarah was a reasonable cook, but when Dave finished a shift, he would often come home to a pile of washing up, and then spend an hour or so cleaning the house. In the end he stopped looking forward to going home at all. No! Whichever way you looked at it, Sarah had become a fat, lazy, whining, manipulative slob, and if he had to choose between telling her so or having an affair, he would choose the affair every time. It was an easy cop-out.

The only problem was Ben and Alice. He adored his kids, and would probably have stayed with Sarah just to be near them. Now he could only see them when she let him, and God only knew what she had been telling them. He tried his best to see them as much as possible and maintain some sort of fatherly role, but Sarah's rigid timetable was not designed to correspond with his shifts at work. He also hated having to pick them up and drop them off at the door with Sarah alternately glowering at him and looking at her watch accusingly. All the fun and spontaneity of fatherhood was ruined for Dave and he knew that his relationship with both Alice and Ben was suffering. Now he was saddled with the mortgage, even though he wasn't living there, and her latest weapon of choice was the CSA. He looked at the photo on his desk of the two blonde, blue eyed children and sighed, then heard someone come in behind him.

He turned and saw the pretty face and fabulous figure of Angela Smith.

"Penny for them?" she said. Dave smiled and tried to get his mind back onto business.

"They aren't worth it!" he replied.

"I heard you were looking for me. What can I do for you?"

"I need a favour. Helen Parrott has come out of her coma and I'm interviewing her at six. I would like to do it with a WPC present."

"OK. Under the circumstances she might feel less intimidated with a woman there," said Angela.

"Not this one!" said Dave. "I might be the one needing protection!" Angela laughed.

"Oh! I see! How is she?"

"She's a tough little cookie. There seem to be no ill effects yet, though she was very tired when I left her."

"That's such a relief though. I only hope she's got something useful to tell us."

"So do I!" Dave's thoughts went immediately to Ed. He really should phone him but he knew that under the circumstances, he should interview her first. As soon as the news was officially out then Helen would be in potential danger.

Helen's face lit up when Dave entered the ward, then fell a little when she spotted Angela behind him. The nurse, Janice, had asked Mary and Dennis to leave them alone for half an hour, so they had gone home to change. Dave pulled two chairs up to the bed and asked Helen how she was feeling.

"Fine!" she answered. "Who's this?"

"I'm WPC Angela Smith. I'm just here two hold his hand and make notes. Don't mind me!"

"I won't!" replied Helen snootily. "Have you brought me anything?" Dave couldn't help smiling, even though he had vowed to keep this interview as routine as possible.

"No! Why? Is there anything you need?"

"I'm desperate for some chocolate, but Mum and Dad only bring me grapes. Look at them! I don't know what they're on. They know I don't eat fruit at home."

"OK," said Dave. "I'll try and remember."

"Aren't my flowers lovely!" said Helen. "Who brought me the roses? They're sweet."

"That was Ed. Edward Curran. He's the man who found you."

"Oh yes!" said Helen excitedly. "Mum told me about him. Can I see him? I want to thank him."

"I expect so," said Dave. "I know he's dying to meet you. I'll try and bring him tomorrow."

"Good," she said. "Aunty Lou says he's really handsome. What happens now?"

"Well, Helen," he said. "I want you to tell me in your own words what happened that night. Why were you on the path so late on your own?"

"I was trying to lose Danny."

"Who's Danny?" asked Dave.

"He gave me a lift into Bournemouth. He lives near our house and he's got a car."

"Is he your boyfriend?"

"No. He acts like he is and everything, but he's a real saddo!"

"So why did you go to Bournemouth with him if he's such a 'saddo'?" asked Dave.

"'Cos I told you. He's got a car," she replied. "He was only supposed to give me a lift but he kept following me round like a flippin' dog. I wasn't going to find a bloke with him hangin' around was I?"

"So what happened?"

"I wanted to tell him to piss off, but I couldn't be horrible 'cos he wouldn't give me a lift again, so I decided to leave and go somewhere else, only when I got outside I saw he'd come after me. I pretended I hadn't seen him and I went round the corner real quick and ducked down round behind the wall of that church. I heard Danny come round the corner but he didn't keep going. Instead he must have stayed where he was 'cos I heard him light a fag, real close, just on the other side of the wall."

"Then what?" asked Dave.

"I waited a few minutes but he didn't go. It was cold and I

was getting fed up so I went quietly up the path."

"Why?" asked Dave. "It doesn't go anywhere."

"It goes up to that big car park," she said. "I know some of the lads who hang out there. I was hoping to scrounge a lift home. Some of them have got really cool cars."

Dave and Angela exchanged a look.

"This Danny," said Dave. "What's his surname?"

"Danny White," she said, then she laughed out loud. "Your not serious! Danny? He couldn't attack a sandwich!"

"We still need to speak to everyone involved. You never know, he might have seen someone hanging about. What's his address?"

"23 Marberry, just round the corner from our place."

"Good. We'll speak to him. Don't worry, we'll be gentle with him," said Dave. "OK, so what happened next?"

"Well. I set off up the path and I saw a wallet on the ground. It had some money in it. I stopped to pick it up and someone jumped out behind me. He forced something soft over my head. Then he put his arm round my neck and forced me backwards into the bushes. I tried to shout but it was hard with that thing over my head. I was so scared." For the first time, Dave could see that her composure was breaking. Her bottom lip quivered as tears started to fill her eyes.

Angela spoke.

"Just take your time Helen. You're being very brave. Try to remember everything as it happened. Any sounds, smells, did he speak at all? I know it's hard but the smallest details are often the most important. Shut your eyes if it helps." Helen nodded and closed her eyes in concentration. Then she opened them suddenly and looked directly into Dave's eyes.

"He laughed! The bastard laughed!" Anger now replaced the tears as her memories sharpened. "It was more like a giggle, or like a snigger. Do you know what I mean?" Both Angela and Dave nodded.

"Did you get the impression that he was fairly young then?" asked Dave.

"I think so."

"Anything else? Anything at all?"

"His arm was very bony and thin. I mean really thin. And he smelt! He smelt like he badly needed a bath, like a tramp or something smells."

"This is great, Helen. Keep going!" She shut her eyes again for a second or two, then continued.

"It must have been a coat or something, the thing over my head. I could feel a zip against my face; it scratched me. I could feel myself being dragged backwards and then I lost my footing. There were leaves and brambles under my hands and he kept pulling me backwards. Then we stopped. I guess we were in the bushes. The next thing I knew he punched me in the stomach. I doubled up and that's when I heard him laugh."

Helen paused a moment and Angela asked if she felt OK to continue. She gulped a breath and carried on.

"After that I couldn't have yelled if I'd wanted to. I didn't have any breath. He forced me to sit on the ground with my back against something cold. It felt like stone. I banged my head hard as he pushed me back. I don't remember much after that."

"Anything at all?" asked Dave. Angela gave him a warning look as Helen was now getting distressed.

"I thought I heard a man's voice in the distance."

"What did it say?"

"I think it was 'hello', but it's not very clear. Then I got a punch in the face through the coat, and he dragged me up and further back. He kept hitting me and hitting me and then he turned me around so that I couldn't see him and took the coat off my head. It was very dark. I felt a hard push between my shoulders and I must have fallen. I don't remember any more."

"Tell me about the wallet."

"It was very old and tatty. The leather felt soft and I think it was brown. I think it had a badge on it or something."

"How big was it?" asked Dave. Helen looked round and picked up one of the envelopes from her 'get well' cards.

"Anyone got a pen?" she asked. Angela passed her the one she was using. Helen thought for a moment and then put pen to paper. What she passed to Dave made his blood run cold.

It was roughly a four inch square with a small circle in the middle. It took Dave a few seconds to find his voice. He looked up at Helen and saw that she was deathly pale, and big fat tears began to slide down her cheeks. He at once felt guilty. He had just made her relive the whole nightmare for the first time since it happened, and shock was finally setting in. He held her hand tightly, and was surprised how cold it felt. He hoped in comparison that his felt warm and strong.

"Thank you Helen," he said. "You are one of the bravest people that I have ever met. I'm sorry we had to put you through that, but you understand why, don't you." Helen nodded. Dave continued. "I just need to talk to my WPC a moment. We won't be long!" Dave nodded to Angela to join him outside.

"What's up?" she said.

"Dave rummaged through his pockets for a second and handed her the drawing from Lou. It was identical. Angela inhaled sharply.

"Where did you get this?"

"A medium gave it me!"

"A what?"

"A medium! You know, a psychic! It was Helen's aunt. They all reckon she's telepathic. She drew this while Helen was still unconscious."

"Christ! Do you believe in all that then?" she asked.

"I dunno," said Dave. "Do you?" Angela just shrugged.

They went back into the ward and found Helen fast asleep.

"Poor thing!" said Angela. "She's exhausted."

"Do you think we pushed her too hard?" asked Dave.

"No. She's a tough little thing! She's got to you hasn't she?"

"Yeah, I guess so. She's a little sod to her parents, but she's so independent, and I think she's coped brilliantly. Do you think she'll be OK?" Angela looked at the sleeping girl, and then back to Dave. Sometimes he was just irresistible. She handed him the notes she had been making.

"I don't doubt it for a minute."

"Sweet dreams," said Dave, before turning and walking out the door.

Dave dropped Angela off at the doors of the station but didn't go in himself. Instead he parked across the road and picked up his mobile phone. It was a relief to know that Ed was definitely out of the frame. Ed's well muscled shoulders and arms definitely didn't fit Helen's description of her attacker, and neither did his standard of personal hygiene.

Dave hadn't seriously doubted Ed's innocence for a moment, but long experience had taught him not to take anything for granted in his line of work. Early on in his career, Dave had found himself shocked at the things that seemingly normal, caring people could do to each other. Now that he had more experience, instinct and gut feeling weren't enough. If he had a hunch he would follow it, but without evidence, intuition was not to be trusted. Police work, especially detective work, became a matter of routine checking, and double checking, every detail. It was often the dullest parts of an investigation which brought results, such as reading endless lists or watching hours of video footage. While he personally trusted Ed, his police training demanded proof.

He dialled up Ed's number and gave him the good news.

"Hi mate! Guess what?"

"What?" replied Ed.

"It's Helen. She's awake and she's OK." The line went silent for a few seconds as Ed tried to take it in.

"Well say something!" said Dave.

"Oh thank God!" said Ed. "When?"

"Earlier today. She's very tired but apart from that she seems fine."

"Can I see her?"

"She's been asking to meet you. How about tomorrow?"

"That would be great, but I'm working all day till four."

"That's OK. As I said, she's very tired at the moment. Tomorrow evening might be better."

"Am I allowed to visit her on my own or would you rather come with me?" asked Ed.

"It's up to you," said Dave, "but I should have told you. Helen has been able to give us a rough description and it puts you out of the frame."

"You mean I'm no longer a suspect?" asked Ed.

"That's right. You're in the clear." Ed was relieved.

"Great! I'll pop along after work. Is there anything she needs?"

"I don't think so. By the way, she loved the flowers." Ed remembered his desperate wish when he bought them; that she should live to see them.

"Good," he said. "Anything else?"

"Oh yes. Chocolate!"

Dave said goodbye and rang off. He found his 'A to Z' in the glove box and looked up Helen's road. Running off the end of it was Marberry Close. Number twenty three must be where this Danny White lived. At last he had a decent suspect, the right age, and in Helen's case, with a possible motive too! He locked up his car and went back to work. Seated at his desk, he checked on the computer whether Danny White had any previous convictions. No luck there, but you couldn't win them all. Then he started typing up the notes from the interview while it was still fresh in his mind. This was his first big break in a high profile case and he had to do everything right. At last he had something to show Mercier.

Chapter 12

Ed sat on his bed and stared at the phone in his hand, even though there was no longer anyone there. He realised that he was shaking and he got up to make himself a cup of coffee. His sense of relief was enormous, and he was desperate to share the good news with someone. But who was there? His first thought was Sharon, but he had made himself vow to stay away for the time being. There was always Pearl, but he would be seeing her tomorrow morning anyway. Of course most people would tell their parents but that didn't apply to him. Since when had they been interested in anything he had to say? He thought of Mike and Trish. Mike would be at work but Trish might be home. He dialled their number but no-one answered. Trish was obviously out. Ed began to feel really sorry for himself; thirty three years old and all alone in the world. It was strange to think that he could disappear tomorrow and no-one would miss him.

The phone in his hand began to ring and poor Ed nearly jumped out of his skin. He pressed answer and said hello. He didn't recognise the number.

"Hi Ed!"

"Hello!" replied Ed. "Who is this?"

"Oh, come on Bruv, it hasn't been that long." Ed was surprised and delighted.

"Sis! How are you? Where are you?"

"I'm staying at Mum and Dad's for a few days." Lara lived

in France with her husband, and only came over once or twice a year.

"How nice for you," said Ed. "Is everything alright at home?"

"Yes, it's fine. Pierre wanted to take the kids to his mother's so I thought I'd take the opportunity to get in some shopping and visit the family, what's left of it."

"How on earth did you get my number?"

"You sent me a letter, remember?"

"Oh yes. Are you phoning from the house?"

"No. I didn't think you'd want me to. Actually I'm at Anne Crabtree's. I saw her in the village and she asked me to phone you. She told me off for not keeping in touch. I didn't know you two were friends." Ed smiled. That sounded like Anne.

"Bless her!" said Ed. "How's Mum and Dad?"

"They're OK. Nothing much seems to change here. They hardly mention you though. Have you fallen out?"

"Not really. When we split up, they took Lisa's side," said Ed. "After that I didn't want to be around them."

"Anne hinted as much. I wish I could have been there for you Ed. It must have been awful."

"Actually, Anne was brilliant. I don't know what I would have done without her. "

"Ed? There's something else. Something I think you should know."

"What's that?" Lara sounded worried. All sorts of doubts filled his mind.

"Lisa has moved her man into the cottage; your darling little cottage!"

"Oh!" was all Ed could manage.

"What do you mean, 'Oh'? Edward! You've got to do something! Mum and Dad are furious."

"Really?" replied Ed. "I'm surprised they haven't invited him around for tea!" Despite his initial outrage at another man living in his house, he found that he wasn't all that bothered. After all, anything that got under his parent's skin couldn't be all bad. Despite himself, he couldn't help asking. "What's he like then?"

"Well he's sort of tall and flashy. He's got a loud voice and says 'Yah' a lot and calls her 'Sweety'. He sort of walks around like everyone is looking at him all the time. Anne reckons he bleaches his hair."

"He sounds perfect for her."

"He's frightful, Ed. Utterly frightful! He's got this really flashy sports car, and he has to fold his knees up round his ears to get into it. He really is the most terrible idiot!"

"Good!" said Ed. "Is Anne there?"

"Yes. Hang on, I'll pass you over."

"Hello Edward. How are you?" It was good to hear Anne's kind, sensible voice again. Ed felt a little guilty at not keeping in touch better.

"I'm fine Anne. How are you?"

"Oh, same as ever. You really are missing the fun and games here you know. The village hasn't had gossip like this since old Nelly Hall ran off with the vicar of St Mary's! Anyway, what have you been up to?"

"Still working. The music is going well. Nothing much to report," he said.

"So you're alright. I do still think about you, you know."

"I know," said Ed, "and thank you."

"I'll pass you back to your sister now," said Anne gruffly. "Bye Edward."

The phone clattered as Anne passed it back to Lara.

"Hi Edward."

"Hi Sis! Listen, how long are you over for?"

"Till Friday. Why?"

"Because I'd like to see you. I've got a lot to tell you but I can't do it over the phone."

"Could I come over on Thursday then," she said. "I'm dying to see where you live."

"That would be great! I've got the day off. Where and when?"

"I've got your address but I don't know if I can find it?"

"Well, I'll meet you in Bournemouth then. What about the Square?"

"OK. Say eleven o'clock!"

"Great! See you then."

"Bye!"

Ed put the phone down and almost immediately it rang again.

"Hello Edward? It's Lou!"

"Hello Stranger! How are you?" said Ed.

"I'm fine," said Lou. " I'm just calling to see if you've heard the news about Helen."

"Yes!" replied Ed. "The police called me a few minutes ago. I'm going to see her tomorrow after work."

"Oh good. Isn't it great that she's going to be alright. Such a relief!"

"I know. The waiting must have been terrible for you."

"And you, Ed. Don't pretend I don't know how worried you were."

"I can't deny it," said Ed. "What can I do for you."

"Well I really phoned to give you the good news, but since you ask?"

"Yes?"

"Would you mind taking me to the hospital with you tomorrow. Only I don't want to go on my own, and my pension doesn't stretch far with all these taxis."

"Of course I will!" said Ed. "Only you've got to promise not to get me into any more trouble!"

"Yes! I'm sorry about that. I'll try to behave, I promise."

"OK," said Ed. "It'll be about four o'clock."

"Fine and dandy!"

Just as he put the phone down it rang again. So much for thinking he was all alone! He looked at the caller display. It was

Trish on her home phone.

"Hello Ed," she said. "Did you call me?"

"Yes, I did!" he replied. "I wanted to tell you that Helen Parrott is awake and she's going to be fine."

"Oh! Thank God for that. Wait till Mike gets home. He'll be so pleased." Ed was touched that she was so genuinely delighted. "In fact," she added, "why don't you come over for dinner tonight and tell him yourself?"

"That would be lovely!" said Ed. "Thank you. Truth be known I could do with the company."

"That's settled then. See you later!"

"Bye!"

That evening passed happily enough. After dinner Trish suggested a game of Monopoly or Trivial Pursuits, but the two lads ended up having a couple of beers and crashing out a few favourites on the guitars, and singing so loudly that they woke the twins. Despite laughing at them, Trish complained that it would have been nice to do something civilised for a change.

The next day Ed went for an early run on the beach, and got to work with ages to spare. Mr and Mrs Patel were delighted at his news. Mr Patel solemnly shook his hand while Pearl gave him a huge hug and a kiss. Their delight was obviously genuine, and Ed reflected once again what thoroughly nice people they were. He told them he was to visit her after work and Pearl suggested that he take some flowers.

"What she really asked for," said Ed, "is some chocolate." Mr Patel spoke up in a rare gesture of generosity.

"Help yourself to any box you like for the young lady," he said. "I insist!" Ed looked at the rather dusty display on the top shelf and inwardly cringed. He had wanted to take her something a bit more special. Mr Patel nodded at him encouragingly, grinning from ear to ear.

"Go on Edward. My treat!"

"Thank you so much!" he said, selecting a boxed assortment

from the shelf. "I'll take her these."

"My pleasure," beamed Mr Patel. Ed popped the box under the counter and started his chores while Mrs Patel was putting the kettle on. She appeared a few moments later with a mug of tea for Ed and some hot buttered toast.

"You eat up Eddie, while it's hot," she said. "We are going to the cash and carry, so you can work in peace and quiet today."

Ed passed the day as usual, dusting, sweeping and serving. He read some magazines and made himself a coffee while they were out, but the day seemed to drag. Mr and Mrs Patel returned in time for The Sweeney again: Ed could hear the brash music blaring out on daytime telly. In the advert break Pearl came out with a large carrier bag and a crafty smile on her face.

"Look what I have found at the cash and carry!" she said. Ed peered into the bag and saw a big box of assorted Swiss chocolates, tied up with a blue and silver ribbon.

"You are to give them to Helen with our love."

"They are lovely Pearl. I'm sure she'll be delighted," he said. "You are so kind!"

"No Eddie, it is you who are kind." She suddenly burst out laughing. "Oh dear! This won't do at all. You are to give her the small box from us and tell her that these are from you. My husband really has no idea you know."

"Oh Pearl! They are exactly what I would have chosen, but I insist that you let me pay for them. I know they weren't cheap."

"No Eddie, it's my treat!"

"I'm sorry, Pearl but I really must pay for them. You do see, don't you?"

"Yes, of course," she said fondly. "Don't worry. I will take them out of your wages."

Ed left the shop at three thirty, dashed home to change, and was outside Lou's bungalow by four. She came out when he beeped, carrying a bag from the greengrocer's. Ed removed the boxes of chocolates from the front seat as she got in.

"Well that's not very healthy!" she said sternly, eyeing up the goodies.

"No. You're probably right," said Ed. "but I was acting on a tip-off!"

"I see," she said. "I expect the poor girl is sick of bloody grapes anyway!" Ed kept quiet and started driving.

Dave followed his road map as he drove, with WPC Angela Smith in the passenger seat beside him. Marberry Close was a quiet cul-de-sac, and he asked Angela to look out on her side as number four flashed past him. He stopped the car opposite number twenty three and looked at it with interest, wondering how close he was to finding his quarry. It looked such an ordinary house; a tidy, white-washed detached, a little bigger than the ones round the corner where Helen Parrott and her family lived. Although it was a fair size it had a rather plain look, as though it may once have belonged to the council. The garden was tidy, as though kept by a conscientious but unimaginative gardener. The drive was a double row of paving slabs with gravel in between running right up the side of the house with enough parking for several cars, although at the moment it contained only one aged dark blue Volvo. The windows on the front of the house still had bare aluminium frames and the only relieving features were the ivy climbing up the wall, and the bright blue painted front door.

"Do you want me to come in with you?" asked Angela.

"Yes. I think it would be best with both of us there," he replied. "We don't know yet what kind of man we're dealing with!"

Ed and Lou entered the hospital and made their way up to the ward. Lou went in first and gave Helen a kiss and a hug while Ed loitered in the doorway. He was surprised at how nervous he felt; far more nervous than he was before a gig. He saw that Mr and Mrs Parrott weren't there and he was glad to have Lou with him. She turned and beckoned him over. Ed approached the bed.

"Hello!" said Helen. She smiled up at him shyly, and like Dave, he was impressed by the startling colour of her eyes. "Are you Edward?"

"That's right. How are you feeling?"

"Oh, I'm OK I suppose. Did you buy me those lovely roses?"

"Yes," said Ed. "They are past their best now. I must get you some more."

"No," she said. "I like these. They are the first thing I saw when I woke up!"

"That's good!" said Ed, feeling foolish for being so awkward.

He noticed that she had one eye on the silver and blue ribboned box he was holding.

"These are for you." Her eyes lit up when she saw what it was.

"Wow! Can I open them now?" He heard Lou grunt behind him as she pulled up a chair and started munching on her own grapes.

"I expect so," said Ed. She started tearing feverishly at the wrappings, then popped one of the glossy brown chocolates into her mouth. Her eyes closed and she murmured as the chocolate melted over her tongue. She finished it with a chew and a swallow, and grinned happily up at Ed.

"That could be twice you've saved my life!" she said. Ed blushed, unsure what to say.

"Told you she was a minx!" muttered Lou. "Pull up a chair, Ed. You might as well sit in comfort while she seduces you."

"Don't be a spoilsport Aunty Lou. Edward saved my life. I should be allowed to show my gratitude you know."

"Just so long as that's all you show him! And his name's Ed!"

"Aunty Lou!" said Helen in mock horror. "It was you who told me how good looking he was."

"Eat your chocolates!" replied Lou, before lapsing back into silence.

"Anyone want one?" said Helen, passing them round. "Go on Ed! You must have one!" Ed took one. It was remarkably good. He enjoyed watching Helen devouring another two or three. It was hard to believe that he was looking at the answer to all his most recent prayers. If the police were right and Ed had disturbed her attacker, then it may well be true that he had saved her life.

He suddenly felt immensely proud of himself, and more than a little protective towards Helen. This was undoubtedly the best, most important thing he had ever done in his life, and it was strange to reflect that if his wife hadn't dumped him, he wouldn't have been at the right place at the right time, and this funny, cheeky little blonde person wouldn't be here at all. He pulled up the remaining chair and settled down for a chat.

Dave rang on the doorbell. There was no answer for a few seconds. He rang again, keeping his finger on the bell a little longer. Eventually he heard a sound from inside, and a man in his dressing gown answered the door. He had obviously been sleeping, and wasn't enjoying being woken up.

"What do you want?" he demanded rudely.

"Police!" said Dave. "PC Warren. WPC Smith. And you are?"

"Arnie White! What's going on?"

"Can we come in please, Mr White?"

"Why? What do you want?" he repeated.

"We are looking for a Daniel White. Is that your son?" Mr White nodded. "We need to talk to him regarding the recent attack on Helen Parrott."

"What's that little whore been telling you," said White.

"Nothing," said Angela. "We are appealing for witnesses and it has come to our attention that your son gave her a lift that night. We are talking to anyone who may be able to help us."

"Well Danny had nothing to do with it. Anyway, he's helping his mother with the shopping. They'll be a while. They've only just gone and I need my sleep. I work nights." They let him run on till he'd finished.

"Well, thank you Mr White," said Dave. "We'll call back later. And sorry to wake you!"

They heard the door slam behind them as they walked back towards the car.

"He seemed a little defensive," said Angela.

"Didn't he just!" replied Dave thoughtfully.

The next morning, Ed had a bit of a lie-in, then got up in time to meet Lara in Bournemouth. He dressed with care, putting on a fresh white shirt and black jeans. He couldn't have his sister thinking he wasn't taking care of himself. It might get back to his mother and father, or even worse, Lisa. He parked as usual at the top car park and walked in. He arrived at the square a couple of minutes early, and settled down to watch the buskers. Lara arrived at five minutes past, and ran up to give him a big hug. He kissed her on the cheek and then she stepped back to get a better look at him.

"I'd forgotten what a good looking brother I have!" she said. "How are you keeping?"

"Oh, quite well. It's very different you know, living in town, but I'm getting used to it."

"I don't know how you stand it. Still, you look great! Shall we find somewhere for a coffee and we can catch up."

"OK. Lead on."

Sharon was also in town that morning. She was feeling a bit down, and part of the reason was Ed. He had definitely been less friendly lately, and she wished she could stop thinking about him, but whichever way you looked at it, she had fallen totally and madly in love. He made her feel special in a way she thought she'd never feel again, and now it seemed he was gone. Another reason for her mood was the fact that Les had started hanging around again. A couple of months ago she would have been glad of the company, but now she knew where her heart lay and, for some reason, having Les around was giving her the creeps. He was undeniably attractive, and despite his 'bad boy' reputation, had always been good to her, but it wasn't enough. It was Ed she needed, and if she couldn't have him then she'd rather be alone.

Today Sharon had decided that what she wanted was a shopping spree. Some new clothes would cheer her up. She couldn't really afford much but there were always the credit cards in a crisis, and she was most definitely having a crisis. As she crossed the square, she caught sight of Ed watching the buskers. It was strange to be able to see him, knowing he was totally unaware that she was there. He looked gorgeous today in his cool white shirt and black jeans, and for a while she thought of just carrying on with her shopping. But that was silly. There was no harm in saying hello. After all, she had to know if they were still friends or not. She plucked up her courage and walked over to him.

Just before she got there, a tall, slim brunette rushed into his arms and he kissed her on the cheek. They stood looking at each other, laughing, clearly pleased to see one another. She was very attractive, and a couple of years younger than Ed. No wonder he didn't want to get too close to Sharon, there was someone else. Why hadn't he just told her? Perhaps he had guessed how she felt and didn't want to hurt her feelings. For God's sake, she was a big girl now. Good looking, single guys didn't grow on trees. Of course he'd have a girlfriend by now; why wouldn't he? She would just have to put Ed behind her and move on, and hope that in time it wouldn't hurt so much. She got out her mobile phone and pressed the redial button.

"Hello," she said "It's me." She listened for a second, then said, "It's about Saturday night. I'd love to come if the offer's still open!"

Lara and Ed settled at a table in Debenham's café and ordered a coffee each. They were still sitting there over an hour later, by which time Ed had finally told her everything. Lara took hold of his hand and said,

"Oh Edward. I can't believe that all this has happened to you in such a short space of time. I think Mum and Dad have been absolutely hateful, and I'll probably tell them so." Ed looked at Lara's serious face and laughed.

"What good would that do?"

"But you've been through all this on your own. I wish you could have told me sooner," she said.

"But we've never really told one another our problems," said Ed. "We just weren't that sort of family."

"No," said Lara, "and it's a shame. It wasn't easy being Mummy and Daddy's precious little pet. I used to envy you having so much freedom."

"And I used to envy you having so much attention."

"It wasn't nice you know. I was so lonely. They drove away most of my friends. Mum found fault with every single one."

"I never knew you were so unhappy," said Ed. "I wish you'd told me!"

"It's a shame we didn't talk like this years ago," said Lara sadly. "I might not have been so keen to move to another country!"

They did a bit of shopping together, mainly stuff for Lara to take home to her family in France. She also stocked up on her beloved 'Marks and Spencer' underwear. They had a final brief hug when they said goodbye, and Ed was sorry to see her go. He felt as though he'd finally got to know his sister for the first time in thirty three years. He felt another small stab of anger towards his parents for letting the family drift so far apart. He hardened his resolve to have very little to do with them in future. If they had indeed driven their precious little Lara into leaving the country, what hope had there ever been for him?

Just over four miles away, at Bournemouth International Airport, a man and a woman stood on the tarmac and watched a slim, white coffin being loaded into a specially chartered plane. They were both sobbing as an airport official solemnly shook hands with them and watched them go aboard. The people in the airport restaurant had a particularly good view of the proceedings on the tarmac. Many had the sensitivity to look away, while others had a good, hard stare. The boy with the mug of hot chocolate sat with his nose an inch from the window, misty patches forming on the glass as he strained to see what was going on. The woman with the black overcoat and the white handkerchief stopped half way up the metal steps and took a final look around. Her gaze seemed to settle for a moment on the boy, who quickly looked down at his mug, turning a furious scarlet. For a moment the room spun around him as his heart beat faster, and he felt as though everyone was looking at him. When he finally looked up, he found the people in the restaurant were going about their business as before and the aircraft was a silver speck disappearing into the horizon, carrying the grieving De Souza family back to their home in Spain.

Chapter 13

It was a Saturday night and Mike and Ed were playing for a huge charity dinner at a beautiful old hunting lodge in the heart of the New Forest. Tonight they were joined by a drummer and a saxophonist from Mikes previous band. It was Ed's first time with a four piece and he was nervous, especially as Mike had decided that they didn't need to rehearse. Louis and Arthur turned up with Mike and they all shook hands. They were dressed alike in black dinner suits, white dress shirts and bow ties, and surprisingly for Ed they were both in their sixties. Unsurprisingly, they turned out to be completely competent, and if anything, Ed felt the odd one out. Mike simply named the next song and nodded to Louis, who counted them in with his sticks.

To start with, the alien sounds of the sax and drums felt intrusive and put Ed on edge, so that he made a few silly mistakes, but he forced himself to relax and soon discovered the true joy of playing in a band. It felt like magic, weaving the sounds together to make music that was far more exciting than anything they had produced as a duo. By the time they stopped for their first break, Ed had a huge respect for the men he was working with and the way they had blended seamlessly together, as naturally as breathing. His obvious enthusiasm amused Mike, especially when he insisted on buying everyone a drink. Ed caught Mike's expression and suddenly realised he was behaving like a mad puppy, so he made the effort to tone it down a little. These guys had probably been doing this since before he was born.

Ed grinned happily into his beer and listened to the gentle banter going on around him as the old friends caught up. It was at this moment that Ed's world collapsed around his ears. Sipping on his pint, his eyes focused on a pair of feet in high, sparkly sandals, feet with tiny palm trees stencilled onto deep red toenails, walking smartly past him towards the bar. He looked up and saw her from behind, a gorgeous curvy figure wrapped in sumptuous burgundy velvet with bare creamy shoulders and short blonde hair. She wore long gold earrings, and a matching fine gold chain round her slender neck. It couldn't be, but it was!

Sharon walked up to the bar where a tall dark-haired man was ordering drinks. Then she caught site of Ed. Her eyes were enhanced with smoky shadow and delicate pink gloss touched her lips. Her dress was cut low at the front showing off a fantastic cleavage. She excused herself from her partner and came over. Ed felt his chest tighten, and momentarily caught Mike's puzzled expression. As he rose to greet her, Sharon's expression remained cool. He led her out into the reception where it was quieter, and gave her a brief peck on the cheek.

"You look sensational!" he said. "What are you doing here?"

"Us council house mum's do get out sometimes you know!" She was cold and cutting and Ed immediately felt hurt. He had never looked down at her; he wasn't exactly in a position to.

"How do you like the band?" he asked, for want of anything better to say.

"Good. Very good." For the first time she smiled. "Look Ed. I just wanted to say thank you."

"What for?"

"Daz has been trying really hard this week. I know that he's got his problems but he said you'd had a talk with him, and he's promised to sort himself out."

"Has he?" said Ed. "I'm glad."

"Good! Well, I'd better let you get back to your friends now. Bye Ed!" She abruptly turned and walked away.

"Sharon!" called Ed on impulse. She stopped. "I only told

him he had a great mum!" Ed felt gutted as she walked on towards the bar without looking back.

Sharon headed straight for the ladies, grateful to find that for the moment she was the only one in there. She looked at her reflection in the mirror, and saw exactly what she was; a frumpy, middle aged mum, tarted up for a night out. Well, if she'd ever had a hope with Ed, she'd just blown it. She dabbed at the tears in her eyes with toilet tissue, drew a deep breath and headed back into the torment that was to be the rest of her evening.

Ed waited a couple of minutes, then headed back to the bar to join the others. Sharon was nowhere in sight.

"Everything alright mate?" asked Mike, unspoken questions in his eyes.

"Oh, it's nothing!" replied Ed, returning to his pint. Hurt as he was, he made a conscious effort to put Sharon out of his mind and concentrate on the job in hand.

Sharon spotted Les at the far side of the ballroom, talking to some people she didn't know, probably about something she wouldn't understand. She wandered over to join him, and the brief smile she received as she approached showed that he hadn't even missed her. Why oh why had she agreed to come? She was like a fish out of water. After a few minutes, the band returned to the stage and Les lead her back to her seat. He finally seemed to notice that she was quiet.

"All right love?" he asked, then turned to talk to the man next to him without waiting for an answer.

Ed was beginning to get back into the swing of the music, and had almost put Sharon to the back of his mind. Mike announced 'Lady in Red', which Ed had to sing. Louis counted them in slowly on his sticks. Suddenly the irony of the song and the words hit him as Sharon and her partner moved onto the floor and started dancing slowly, right in front of him. For a moment he almost completely lost it, and looked wildly around. He found Mike right by his side, who had summed up the situation and was there, giving him confidence and willing him on. Mike spoke the words of the next line to him and Ed managed to sing them, hardly missing a beat. He nodded his thanks to Mike and picked up the song once more, shutting out everything else firmly from his mind.

Sharon was grateful that their table was near the back of the ballroom so that she could remain unseen from the stage. The hurt look in Ed's eyes was still haunting her and she knew that she had behaved badly. She didn't know why she had been so cutting; it had just come out. Still, he'd get over it. He had the lovely brunette to fall back on. Maybe she was in his bed right now, waiting for him to get home. It was at this moment that the music slowed down and Les decided that it was time to give her some attention. He stood up and asked her to dance. Sharon tried to refuse but Les was not one to take no for an answer, and he lead her firmly by the elbow onto the dance floor.

For a fleeting moment her eyes met Ed's and he suddenly seemed to forget his words. Sharon wanted the ground to swallow her up as she was steered to a space right at the front, then she saw the bass guitarist walk over beside him and say something. Ed seemed to find his place and thankfully he carried on. Sharon was forced to dance only feet away from the man she loved, while another man pressed his body against her, swaying in time to the music. She could feel his excitement rising and suddenly realised with horror that he would expect her to go home with him. This was the middle of the forest. She could hardly get a taxi. Meanwhile, the sound of Ed's soft, warm voice filled her head, filling her with regret and longing. This was all wrong. What was she doing? Filled with despair she submitted to Les's attentions and waited in dumb agony for the end of the song.

While Ed was packing up the gear he guessed that Mike

wanted to talk to him, but knew that he wouldn't in front of the others. The house lights had been raised and people were leaving in droves. Ed had lost sight of Sharon and her partner. He cursed himself for not getting a better look at the man, and hoped against hope that she wasn't still involved with Les.

It took about twenty minutes for all the speakers, stands, amps and leads to be packed away in their correct cases. This done, Ed and Mike went outside to collect their cars. A light drizzle was falling, and the forest around them looked hazy and surreal in the diffused lights.

"Do you want to tell me about it?" asked Mike.

"Not right now thanks," said Ed, "but sorry for losing it back there."

"Hey!" said Mike. "You did OK! I know that Louis and Arthur are really impressed with you. If it's alright with you, I'd like to go out as a four-piece more often." Ed smiled back at him.

"That would be great!"

"OK! I'll fix it up." Mike went off to find his car, wondering exactly how much to tell Trish.

Sharon had found her coat and was waiting in the foyer of the hotel, while Les was making a phone call on his mobile in the bar. Who on earth could he be calling at this time of night? Eventually he reappeared and strode up to her, taking both her hands in his.

"Listen honey," he said. "Something's come up! I've got to go and see someone. I'm really sorry. I wouldn't do this if it wasn't important. I've called you a taxi; here's the money." He shoved forty quid in her hand, pecked her on the cheek and was gone. Bloody cheek! She was both angry and relieved. Well at least it solved one problem. Disconsolately she wandered outside just in time to see the rear lights of Les's powerful car disappear into the gloom. It had come on to drizzle and Sharon let the cold wet droplets fall onto her upturned face. She wondered if she really cared about anything any more.

A few minutes later, both cars were loaded up in the car park behind the hotel, and Louis and Arthur shook hands with Ed, then climbed in with Mike, who waved and drove off. He had asked Ed to call him in the morning and Ed promised he would. His red BMW was waiting patiently and Ed climbed in out of the damp, started his engine and roared out of the gravel car park and across the front of the hotel, heading for home. No matter how he was feeling, his beloved car always gave his spirits a lift. It had become part of him, almost a symbol of his new found freedom.

Suddenly his eyes caught a figure standing in the rain, just outside the foyer. Ed continued on, replaying the fleeting scene over in his mind. It couldn't be. Suddenly he slammed on the brakes. He had to be sure. Carefully turning the car round, he headed back to the hotel. There she was, a figure wrapped in a dark fur coat with short blonde hair and sparkly sandals. He stopped the car in the middle of the road and got out. She saw him and walked over.

"Get in!" he shouted. It was raining properly now and she was getting soaked. He opened the door for her, and she climbed in. Her lovely spiky hair had flopped and her mascara had started to run down her face. He didn't know what to say so he turned the heater on and just drove. He needed to keep his attention on the road as it was pitch black outside and the New Forest ponies wandered into his path with only their eyes and their reflective collars showing in the headlights. After a while he saw that it wasn't rain, but tears sliding down her face. He pulled the car over on a grass verge and cut the engine.

"Sharon. I need to know what's going on," he said gently. "I don't understand any of this, but I wish you'd let me help." She remained silent but fresh tears ran down her cheeks.

"Who was that man?"

"Les," she whispered. Ed's blood ran cold. He fought to

contain his emotions, remembering his promise to Daz.

"Are you back together?" he asked, almost dreading the reply. At last she spoke.

"I don't know. He wants to buy a big house where he says we can live as a family. He wants me to give up my job and work for him. He says he wants to look after me."

"It's not a bad offer," said Ed. "What's the problem?"

"Oh Ed!" She turned her tear-stained face towards him in the dark car. "He's not you!" Then she broke down and wept, while Ed held her as best he could, shocked and confused. He didn't know what to say. He had promised himself not to get involved. But Sharon was a friend, and he couldn't watch a friend walk blindly into the lion's den, possibly ending up in deep trouble, or even prison? He held her tightly and waited for her sobbing to subside.

"I'm sorry," she said finally, lifting her head. "I shouldn't have said that."

"Which bit?"

"The bit about you," she replied. "It's all right. I know you've got a girlfriend."

"Then you know more I do!"

"But I saw you in Bournemouth together," she said. "She had long dark brown hair and a red jacket!" Ed laughed out loud.

"That's my sister, Lara! For goodness sake! Is that what this is all about?"

"But I saw you hug and kiss her. You must be very close!"

"On the contrary, she lives in France. That was the first time I had seen her in ages."

"Oh Ed! I feel such a fool. Do you know I only went back to Les to get over you?"

"But why do you need to get over me?" asked Ed in amazement.

"Look at me!" she cried. "As if a gorgeous bloke like you would ever look at me?"

"Well, this bloke is looking at you; has been for ages." He leant forward and gently kissed her on the lips. She gasped and pulled away and for a moment their eyes met. Then Sharon pulled him close and kissed him as though her life depended on it. In all his life Ed had never known such a kiss. The force of her passion was wild and exciting, and at last Ed had to pull away to draw breath. He gently stroked his index finger down the side of her face and laughed, his eyes sparkling and said,

"Well! What do we do now?" She leant over and snuggled her head into his shoulder.

"What I suggest, " she said. "is that we go back to your place and shag our brains out. Then we can discuss the rest in the morning!"

"I guess that would be a fairly good plan," said Ed. "Hold on to your seat, you shameless hussy!"

Dave Walker was possibly the only officer who actually liked the night shift. It was four thirty in the morning and the rain had finally stopped, leaving the air damp and hazy. He was in the panda with PC Sam Wallis, a tall blonde lad in his early twenties, who was yawning widely when the message came over the radio. They had been stationed in the town centre but it was fairly quiet for a Saturday night, probably due to the weather. Dave ignored it till the address registered something in his brain. There was a fire at Ed's house. He pointed to the radio and said to Sam,

"Respond to that! I know who it is!" Sam told the operator that they were attending while Dave put his blue lights on and his foot down. When he got there he saw that it wasn't the house but the garage that was on fire. The fire engine had beaten him to it, and huge jets of water were pouring through the gaps where the doors and the window used to be. Dave could just make out patches of red paint, the colour of Ed's BMW. He left the scene and made his way round to the front door with Sam following. He pressed the bell with number five on and waited.

Sharon woke with a shock to the piercing sound of Ed's doorbell. Ed sat up with a start, and was immediately aware of a change. There were flashing lights outside his window and strange sounds all around. He grabbed his shirt and said to Sharon,

"Stay there!" He ran down and opened the door and was surprised to see Dave. His first thought was that he was going to be arrested again, but then he smelt the smoke and said,

"What's happening?"

"I'm sorry mate," said Dave. "Your car's on fire!"

"No!" shouted Ed, and ran out in his bare feet. The flames were nearly out but Ed couldn't see his car. The garage roof had fallen in, the double doors were completely gone and all that was left was an evil smelling pile of blackened bricks and soggy timbers.

"Not my BM!" he said, shaking his head. Sharon had come to join him, wearing Ed's dressing gown and sparkly sandals. She looked at the scene in horror and put a hand on his shoulder.

"Oh my God, Ed! What happened?"

"I don't know!" They stood and watched for a while till the embers had died out and then Dave went and had a word with the fire officer in charge. A small crowd had gathered on the pavement including the landlord, Mr fellows, who was shaking his head sadly at the devastation. Eventually Dave came over and relayed what the fireman had told him.

"They say there is no way this was an accident. I'm afraid it's arson, Ed. You'd better tell me who you've been upsetting lately."

"I've no idea!" said Ed. "Christ Dave! Who would do this?"

"You've really no idea at all? Shame though. It was a nice car. I hope you're well insured."

"Yes, fully comp. Shit! I left my amp in the boot!" Dave looked around and then said quietly to Ed,

"Don't make it obvious but have a look round and see if there is anyone watching who you recognise. Some people like to see the results of their handiwork."

Ed glanced discretely around the small crowd but no-one caught his attention.

"Can't see anyone! I suppose if they are still here, they'll be hiding."

"Yeah," said Dave. "Or they've done a runner!" He looked at Sharon and said, "Aren't you going to introduce me then?"

"Oh yes! Sorry! This is Sharon, a very good friend. Sharon; this is PC Dave Walker, old school friend and reprobate."

They solemnly shook hands and Dave said,

"Nice outfit!" Sharon looked down and replied cooly,

"Thanks!"

They watched the fire crews leave and Ed suddenly realised he was shivering like mad. Dave told them to go back to bed and he would come and see them in the morning.

"Have a good think about who could have done this," he said. "It looks personal to me." Both Sharon and Ed thought of Les but neither said anything. Ed wandered over to look at his car, but another police officer told him to stay back. Sharon came up beside him and squeezed his arm.

"Come on," she said. "You're frozen." Ed stayed where he was, looking in dismay at the wreckage.

"What am I going to do?"

"Don't worry. We'll sort something out. Come back to bed." This time she steered him firmly towards the house. Dave was talking to Mr Fellows as they left. The air was damp and heavy with the acrid smell of burning, and PC Sam Wallis was busy taping off the area.

Once inside, Sharon put the kettle on while Ed sat miserably on the edge of the sofa. She pulled a blanket off the bed and put it round his shoulders, snuggling up to him while the kettle boiled.

"Are you OK?" she asked gently.

"Yeah! Sorry love, I'm fine."

"Penny for them then!"

"I was just wondering who could have done this," he said. "How much do you know about Les?"

"I knew you would think of him!"

"Well how much do you really know about him?"

"OK!" she said. "I know he's got some pretty hard friends, and to be honest if he knew about us I wouldn't put it past him, but how would he know?"

"It seems unlikely. We certainly weren't followed through the forest."

"Besides Ed, it isn't really his style. He's more likely to walk up and punch you than burn your car in the dead of night!"

"Oh that is reassuring!" said Ed.

"No! I mean that this seems sort of cowardly. Do you know what I mean!"

Ed did know what she meant. Suddenly he thought of Daz, who was known to lurk the streets in the dark, and who was also cowardly and bitter. He pushed the thought out of his mind and sipped hot tea from the mug she handed him, his shivers finally subsiding.

"Aghhh!!!" Sharon had finally caught sight of herself in the mirror. "I can't believe I've been walking around outside looking like this!" Her mascara had reached the area around her chin and her hair was stuck up on one side and flat on the other.

"Don't worry dear!" he said. "It was quite dark!"

"Oh my God! Your mate Dave! And all those firemen!"

"Yes," said Ed. "What a wasted opportunity!"

"That's not what I meant and you know it," she replied crossly. "Come back to bed if you've finished your tea.

"How could I resist?"

Dave and Sam got into the squad car and made their way back to the station. Mercier wasn't in yet so they got a coffee from the machine and sat at Dave's desk. The place was really quiet as most of the night shift weren't back in yet.

"OK, so tell me what was so interesting about that case?" said Sam.

"What do you mean?" asked Dave innocently.

"I know you! You're on to something!"

"Maybe. It's these attacks on women in Bournemouth. You know, the De Souza murder case!"

"What about it?" asked Sam.

"I'm not sure. It's just that my friend Ed keeps popping up."

"But we've ruled him out as a suspect, haven't we?"

"Oh yes, it's not him. I'd bet my pension on it," said Dave. "I've just got this feeling that he's the key to the whole thing."

"Do you want to bring him back in for questioning?"

"No," said Dave. "He doesn't know anything. Call it instinct if you like but there's a link there somewhere; we've just got to find it."

"And how are you going to do that?"

"I don't know, but he's involved," said Dave stubbornly. "You mark my words!"

Chapter 14

The next morning, Ed woke up slowly from a deep sleep and realized that there was another body squashed into his single bed with him. He opened his eyes and saw the back of her short blonde hair and smiled as he remembered the night before. Then, with a jolt, the tragedy of his car came back to him and he wanted to leap out of bed and check that it was real, but he didn't want to disturb Sharon so he lay still, turning over all the possibilities in his mind. It seemed so crazy, so far fetched. If it was Les, then that didn't make much sense. He hadn't been that bothered about Sharon the night before, and what kind of man would leave a woman to get herself home from the middle of the forest at that time of night anyway? Certainly not a possessive one! If it was possible to dislike someone any more then he did already, then his opinion of Les plummeted.

What about Daz? He had to be the favourite. But he couldn't quite see him being brave enough, even though he was certainly stupid enough. Added to that, whoever did this must have had patience and organisation; not two words he would have willingly applied to Daz. He was spoilt and childish, and had a nasty temper when things weren't going his way, but whoever did this was cold and calculating, and let's face it, Daz would probably have got himself caught. It occurred to Ed that he had only two possessions that really mattered to him, his car and his guitar, and that suggested only two possibilities. Either this was a totally random attack by some crazy pyromaniac, or else it was someone who knew him very, very well. The thought suddenly made Ed shiver and he felt Sharon begin to stir.

It was eleven thirty on a Sunday morning and Daniel White had been brought in for questioning. Dave had only had a few hours sleep and wasn't feeling very merciful. He realized that he had probably breathed in a lot of smoke the night before which might account for the headache and the slightly sick feeling which even the canteen coffee couldn't shift. He was sitting on the right hand side of Inspector Mercier, whose strong, cheap after shave wasn't helping. Danny white had come with them voluntarily. His father had answered the door first and was sloppily dressed in his night clothes as before. He had refused to let them see Danny, and had started to shout the odds about police harassment and the like, when Danny suddenly appeared calmly beside his father wearing outdoor shoes and carrying a mack. He said that he was ready to go, and that he wanted to help in any way he could. In fact he seemed quite glad to escape.

Danny White was almost six feet tall and built like a beanpole. He had an open, amiable face, and a sort of hopeful expression. He was wearing dated drainpipe jeans and a striped T-shirt with an open collar, and if pressed to describe him, Dave would have labelled him a bit of an 'anorak'. His willingness to be questioned and his eagerness to help were giving Dave his first doubts about his prize suspect. The only thing that Dave did notice in the car however was the faint sour smell of body odour.

When they arrived at the station, Dave took Danny in the back way from the car park and showed him into the interview room where Mercier was waiting. They shook hands and he introduced himself.

"Now, Mr White," said Mercier. "We are thankful for your co-operation and want to stress that you are not under arrest, and that you are free to go at any time. Do you understand?"

"Oh yes!" said Danny.

"Before we start," said Mercier, "is there anything we can get you?"

"Yes please! I'd like some tea?" Mercier looked at Dave, who got up and said,

"Good idea! Sir?"

"Yes please, Constable Walker. No sugar! We'll suspend the interview till you get back."

"Two sugars for me please!" added Danny. Dave plodded off to get the teas thinking that it would have been easier if they had arrested the bugger. At least they could have cut straight to the chase without all the niceties, and he wouldn't be getting treated like the flamin' tea boy.

When he returned, Danny and Mercier were discussing, of all things, the weather. He reflected that this was probably the limit of Mercier's social niceties, and carefully handed round the teas. At least they had waited for him to start, and he popped a new tape into the machine.

"I say," said Danny. "Do you have to record this?"

"No?" replied Mercier. "It's just that Constable Walker here is the kind of chap who likes to keep a record of everything. Bit of a stickler, ha ha! You don't mind do you?" Dave knew that Mercier badly wanted the interview on tape and had managed to neatly side-step the question, so he kept quiet and smiled at Danny apologetically.

"No, no! By all means, go ahead. I'm sure you chaps know exactly what you're doing."

"OK Danny," said Mercier in a voice that was as encouraging as he could muster. "Tell me in your own words exactly what happened on the night in question, starting with the moment when Helen Parrott asked you for a lift."

It was over an hour later when Danny White had finished telling his story, in painfully minute detail. Dave was close to dropping off. The highlight of the hour had been when he'd had to change the tape. Danny on the other hand looked as though he had enjoyed himself thoroughly. He clearly saw himself in the role of star witness, although he actually had nothing useful to tell them at all. This was the most exciting thing that had happened to him in years and he was enjoying the attention. His story tallied perfectly with the one that Helen told, and both Dave and Mercier began to think it was hopeless when there was a tap on the door.

"Come in!" called Mercier. The door opened and WPC Angela Smith put her head in.

"Excuse me sir! Could I have a word?"

"Of course. Excuse me for just a moment."

He returned a couple of minutes later with Angela, and said,

"Right Mr White! You are free to go. If you wouldn't mind waiting with WPC Smith a moment, I'll find someone to drive you home." He nodded to Dave to follow him out and they went along the corridor and into an office, out of hearing. Mercier leant back against the desk and folded his arms in front of him, looking sternly at the younger officer.

"OK, Dave lad. What did you make of that?"

"Well to be honest sir, I wouldn't like to hazard a guess, but frankly he doesn't look like he's got it in him."

"He could just be a good actor," suggested Mercier. "Anything else?"

"He's the right build I suppose, and he does have a slight freshness problem, but if it was Danny, I think Helen would have recognised him."

"Mmm," said Mercier. "I'm inclined to agree. By the way, that Angela Smith is a bright girl!"

"Oh? What has she found?"

"Did you know that the father has a record?"

"No!" said Dave, his ears suddenly pricking up. "What for?"

"ABH and assault! Charges were brought by the wife in 1998. Also he was caught in possession of some illegal imported videos back in the eighties."

"Now that is interesting," said Dave thoughtfully.

It was left to Angela and Dave to drive Danny home. Before they reached the car, Dave had a sudden thought.

"Hey, Danny!" he said. "Do you carry a wallet?"

"Yes, of course!" said Danny, looking puzzled. "Why?"

"Would you mind letting me see it."

"What on earth for?" asked Danny.

"Please? Just humour me!" Danny shrugged and pulled a wallet from his jeans back pocket, a hideous affair of royal blue nylon and black velcro.

"Is that the only one you own?" Dave made sure he was looking Danny straight in the eye as he asked the last question. Danny nodded emphatically, with a look of bewilderment on his face.

"Don't you want to open it?" he asked, puzzled.

"No thanks," said Dave. "You can put it away now."

"OK!" and he carefully replaced it in the back pocket of his jeans.

After they had dropped Danny off at his gate, Dave had a long, hard look at the house.

"What do you make of the father?" he asked.

"Might be worth looking into," said Angela. "There may be a connection."

"I've been wondering why young Danny was so keen to come to the station. Suspects don't usually throw themselves into our arms!"

"Perhaps he was keen to do his civic duty. He seems fond enough of Helen."

"Or perhaps he was told to keep us out of the house," said Dave thoughtfully. "Maybe there's something we weren't supposed to see!" He lapsed into silence for a while then Dave noticed the curtain move in an upstairs window. He nudged Angela and she followed his gaze. Arnold White's angry face looked out at them, then he grabbed the curtain and pulled it shut. Dave laughed.

"Well! For whatever reason, we seem to have rattled his cage. Angie?" he said. "What was the name of the first victim? You know, the young girl who belted him and ran away."

"I'm not sure," she replied. "Wasn't it Kelly or something?"

"That's it! Kelly Foster! Could you radio through and find out her address? I need to check something out and I'd like you to be with me."

Ed handed Sharon a steaming mug of tea, then ran his hand through her messy, blonde hair. She sat up in bed and looked at him with concern.

"Are you alright?" she asked.

"Yeah, I guess I'm OK. You?" She nodded and sipped her tea.

"I was just thinking," she said. "What are you going to do about a car."

"I don't know. I might have enough left to buy an old banger. It'll be ages before the insurance comes through."

"Phone the insurance company this morning anyway," she said. "They might be able to help."

"Let me wake up a bit first. It hasn't quite sunk in yet." Ed's mobile began to ring on the coffee table. It was Mike.

"Morning Ed! Just phoning to see what you thought of last night." Ed dragged his mind back to the gig. It seemed like light-years ago.

"Fantastic! Louis and Arthur are the business."

"I think so! I'll phone them and thank them tonight. Trish wants to know if you're coming over for lunch?"

"Er, it might be difficult today. Tell her thank you but I'd better leave it."

"Alright. Are you OK, mate? Is there someone there with you?"

"Yep!" replied Ed.

"Anyone I know?"

"Yep! Sort of!"

"Not that blonde bird from last night?"

"Yep!" replied Ed again.

"In that case I'll leave you to it."

"Before you go," said Ed, "I'd better give you the bad news." He told Mike all about the fire the night before.

"Oh my God!" said Mike in horror. "Are you staying in for a while?"

"I expect so," said Ed. "I've got to wait for the police to come back."

"OK! I'm on my way round. Don't go anywhere, I've got an idea!" and before Ed could protest he was gone.

"Well well!" said Ed to Sharon. "It looks like you're about to meet my best mate. He's on his way round!"

"Crikey!" said Sharon. She jumped out of bed and started gathering her clothes from where they had fallen in their haste the night before. Ed watched in amusement as she shook out her ball gown, then looked at him in horror.

"I can't wear this!" she cried.

Ed laughed and calmly opened his wardrobe and took out a clean pair of running trousers, thanking his lucky stars that he had been to the launderette a couple of days before. Then he chose a clean a T shirt from the drawer.

"Put these on," he said. "They should be OK!"

"Thanks!" she said. "That'll be the second time in twelve hours that I've got in your trousers!" Ed grinned at her shyly. Sex the night before had been great. Ed had never realized that it could be so much fun. Sharon's lovely, curvy body had fitted so snugly against his, and she knew how to turn him on something rotten. Their lovemaking had been more erotic and exciting than anything Ed had ever experienced, and when they finally reached climax, they made it together. Afterwards they had cuddled up with Ed gently stroking her naked skin, till she had shivered and pulled the duvet up over them. He watched her now, putting on his ill-fitting clothes and said,

"Do you know? You even look sexy in that!" He walked over and put his arms round her waist. She slid round to face him and they started kissing passionately again.

Suddenly the doorbell shrilled, making them both jump out of their skins.

"That f—ing bell!" said Ed crossly. He gave her a swift kiss on the lips, then went down to see who it was while Sharon searched for his comb. To his surprise he found Pearl on his doorstep.

"Oh Eddie! I'm so sorry to hear about your car! Are you alright?"

"Yes Pearl. I'm fine, but how did you know?"

"Mr Fellows told me when he came in for his morning paper. He was ever so upset."

"Yes. I suppose he would be; it was his garage. I must go and see him."

"The thing is Eddie, me and Asif, we want to help!"

"That's very kind," said Ed, "but I don't think there's much that can be done."

"Well we thought that this might be of some use to you, just till you get another one of your own. I know it's not as good as what you're used to but...." She stepped back, and behind her he could see Mr. Patel looking anxiously from the driving seat of an old, sky blue Vauxhall Nova in gleaming condition.

"Where did you get it?" asked Ed in amazement. Mr Patel got out of the car, walked slowly up the uneven path and self-consciously shook hands with Ed.

"A couple of years ago my wife was complaining about having to go everywhere in the front of the van, so I bought this as a surprise. We used it a lot for the first few weeks but now we only save it for best. I have cleaned it this morning and the tank is full of petrol." Ed's eyes filled with tears though he didn't know why, and he hugged the two kind people who clearly thought so much of him.

"I don't know what to say!" he said. "Thank you!"

"So you will take it then?" said Mr Patel eagerly.

"Yes please. Just till I can replace mine." The elderly couple seemed genuinely pleased that he had accepted their offer and he was touched to see them walking home, hand in hand.

He went back upstairs to Sharon, who seemed to have sorted out her hair and face a little.

"Where were we?" he asked, pulling her towards him.

"Who was at the door?" she asked.

"The Patels," he replied, and told her what they had done. She was pleased and surprised.

"They must think an awful lot of you to trust you with their precious car."

"I know. I just wish I had a garage to keep it in." He slipped his arms round her waist and nuzzled into her neck, just as the doorbell rang again.

"Bugger!" he said.

This time it was Mike.

"Come in," said Ed. "We were just about to make some coffee."

"Are you sure? I don't want to intrude."

"Of course. Anyway, Sharon wants to meet you!" Ed stood back to let Mike in but he stayed where he was.

"Before you go up, I wondered if you could use this?" Ed looked out and saw Mikes car parked behind the Nova. Surely not another car? He followed Mike round to the back and watched as he opened the boot. In the back was a large black amplifier, two small speakers and a carrier bag full of leads. Ed's mouth fell open. It was a far better PA system than he had been using.

"Where did you get all this?" asked Ed. Mike grinned.

"You haven't seen the inside of my garage, have you mate? I bought this lot nearly ten years ago from a bloke in my band, just to help him out like, but it's hardly been used. I keep it as a spare, but to be honest, you may as well hang on to it if you can use it!"

"It's just what I need, but I couldn't possibly keep it!"

"Well, see how you get on with it first," said Mike. "If you like it then maybe you can buy it off me. I'd let you have it cheap and you could pay me monthly or something if you'd rather."

"Cheers mate," said Ed happily. "Come on in!" Things were working out better and faster than he had dared to hope.

Kelly Foster and her family lived in a house about half a mile on the far side of Bourneside Park. It was a pleasant, tree lined road in a quiet residential area and the large house they occupied was split into two spacious flats. The Fosters lived in the ground floor flat overlooking a well tended garden. Apparently Mr Foster was a salesman who stayed away from home a lot. However, today he answered the door.

"Yes?" he inquired politely.

"We're sorry to bother you on a Sunday, Mr Foster," said Dave, holding out his warrant card. "We just wondered if it was possible to have a quick word with Kelly."

"Yes, by all means. She's in her bedroom, though God only knows what state she's in. She hasn't surfaced yet!"

"That's alright, Mr Foster. We'll try not to keep her. It's just that I want to double check one small detail with her."

"I suppose it's about this awful mugging. Please come in. Would you like my wife to get you a tea or a coffee?" He showed them into a large lounge with two bay windows overlooking the lawn.

"No thank you," said Angela. "What a lovely room. The gardens look delightful."

"So they should. We pay a fortune to the blasted management company to keep them that way. I'll go and fetch Kelly for you."

It was a couple of minutes before Kelly showed up, and she had clearly just jumped into the first jeans and T shirt that she could find as they were all creased.

Her long, shiny hair was freshly brushed and loose on her shoulders, and her clear freckly skin didn't have a trace of make-up, making her look very young and vulnerable.

"Hello Kelly," said Dave. "How are you?"

"I'm OK," she replied shyly.

"Have you got over your fright yet?" asked Angela with concern.

"I'm OK now I suppose. It all seems a little scary, like a bad dream. I have been wondering something though."

"What's that?"

"The man who attacked me. Is he the one who killed that Spanish girl?" Dave looked at Angela, hoping she would answer.

"We're not sure, Kelly," she said gently. "It's possible."

"We are still trying to establish a link." Dave added. "That's why we are here Kelly. Have you remembered anything else? Anything at all?" Kelly looked down and shook her head.

"I wish I could," she said, "But there was nothing. It all happened so quickly."

"Think back to the very first thing," said Dave. "What were you doing the moment before you were grabbed." Unfortunately no-one had seen Mrs Foster enter the room.

"Is this really necessary?" she asked testily. "Can't you see you're upsetting her?" Dave could have strangled the woman.

"It's OK Mum. I want to help!" said Kelly.

"Think hard, Kelly," urged Angela. Kelly looked down again. Dave prayed for Mrs Foster to keep quiet for just a little longer.

"I was just walking along. Then I bent down to…. Oh my God! I've just remembered. The wallet!"

Ed, Sharon and Mike sat in the bedsit, drinking coffee and chatting on the sofa. To Ed's relief, the other two seemed to be hitting it off. Mike was telling her about the twins and Sharon was listening and laughing.

"They sound a right handful!" she said. "How lovely to have twins."

"Have you got any kids?" asked Mike.

"Yeah. Just the one and he's all grown up now!"

"Really?" said Mike. "You don't look old enough. What's his name."

"Daz! Well, Darius really."

"Darius?" said Ed in surprise. "I didn't know that!"

"What did you think Daz was short for?" asked Sharon.

"Oh I don't know!" said Ed. "Darren or Darryl or something I suppose. I hadn't given it much thought."

"What's he like?" asked Mike, innocently. Ed and Sharon looked at each other and smiled.

"A right pain in the arse!" she said, and they left it at that.

When Mike rose to leave, they went down with him to inspect the damage. Ed led them round the back of the house, and the awful scene of devastation that met their eyes stopped them all in their tracks.

"Holy shit!" said Mike. For a start, the smell was appalling, and the extent of the damage was horribly clear in the daylight. Ed could just make out a couple of glimpses of red paint, but most of his beautiful BMW was black and blistered, and almost distorted out of recognition. The blackened bricks and timbers bore ample witness to the ferocious heat of the night before, and the subsequent rain had left the whole scene looking eerie, damp and depressing.

A few minutes earlier, life hadn't seemed all that bad to Ed. Sure, he had lost his precious car, but he had found himself surrounded by friends with kind offers of help.

Added to that, his love life was definitely on the up. He had just had terrific sex with a terrific woman, who gave every indication of wanting to stick around, and to top it all, he had just had his first gig with a proper band. Yes, life wasn't all bad.

But looking round him now, he was reminded once again that someone was out to get him, and that someone was pretty serious.

Chapter 15

A fortnight had passed since the killing of Claudia De Souza and the police were still no nearer to finding the culprit. A meeting had been called for ten o'clock that morning and the incident room was crowded with uniform and CID, cradling mugs of machine coffee and waiting for the top man to arrive. There was the constant hum of conversation and speculation, but still no hard evidence. That was the trouble with this kind of case; if the attacks were completely random then it was useless looking for a pattern; there was none to find. Plus if the attacker was previously unknown, and this one was possibly quite young, then the clues wouldn't lead anywhere till he got himself noticed or made a mistake. If he played it safe and lay low for a bit then it could take months to earth him out. But earth him out they would.

The hum of conversation died down as the top brass entered the room, and cigarettes were hastily stubbed out in ashtrays that shouldn't be there. Mercier started by giving a report on the progress so far, then he called on the various officers following separate lines of enquiry to summarise their investigations, thus pooling all the information. Dave had been checking up on Danny and Arnold White, and a search had been done on their home. This had been fruitful in disclosing the fact that Mr White senior had once again involved himself in the illegal videos game, with the difference that this time the pornographic material had been recorded on DVD. However, there was still no lead into the murder enquiry. Investigations were continuing but Dave wasn't hopeful that any link would be found.

They heard long reports from 'scene of crime' officers, forensics and pathology. Expanded photos in glorious technicolour were pinned to the walls, giving fresh reality to the flagging investigation, and were being studied and discussed in great detail by various experts. They had called in a psychologist to put together some sort of profile, and had also received the news that the Spanish police were sending someone over to check on their progress. Mercier had managed to resist the move up till now as he didn't relish the prospect of a stranger, and a foreigner to boot, interfering in 'his' investigation.

Now the visit was inevitable and Mercier had to accept it with gracious defeat. Heaven knows, they weren't getting very far on their own, and a fresh pair of eyes from a complete outsider could cast a whole new light on the enquiry. Dave had managed to avoid any further involvement for Ed, but had imparted the information that a psychic had given him a description of a penknife. As expected, this was received with doubt, and a little mirth, from his fellow officers and it was unlikely to be followed up. At least now his information was out in the open and he had nothing more to hide. Another main subject for discussion was the wallet, which the attacker seemed to be using as some sort of bait to stop his victims. Eventually the meeting was winding up and officers were being assigned their new lines of enquiry. Everyone suddenly looked busy and the incident room started to clear.

Sharon and Ed had been together for a whole week now, and were getting on famously. Life was good and Ed had never felt so wanted and loved in his life. They had mainly slept apart most nights for the simple reason that Ed only had a single bed, and they needed to sleep sometime. Also, they didn't want to rub Daz's nose in it too much yet. In time he may be able to accept them as a couple but for now Ed was receiving the silent, moody treatment. On reflection Daz could have behaved much worse and they both thought that it would only be a matter of time before he got used to this new situation. It was strange for all of them, not least of all Ed.

When he had met Lisa, he had first adored her from afar, then had eventually asked her for a date. He thought she was the most beautiful thing he had ever seen and had been the proudest man alive when she had eventually agreed to marry him. But still there had been a feeling that she had bestowed on him a great favour, and throughout their marriage the feeling of condescension had been allowed to continue. With Sharon there was real partnership, and deep understanding. Maybe age and experience had played their part, and the knowledge that not everything was for keeps. Life had to be lived for the here and now. Ed would always look back on those days as a time of sunlight and laughter, of sex and fun, a time when they thought that nothing could damage this perfect little world that they had created. As for Sharon, she had got what she wanted; a kind, handsome man who clearly adored her and treated her well. But with Ed it was so much more than that. For the first time in her life she knew she had someone who she trusted, who would never let her down. Although she had only known him for a short while, Sharon believed with her whole heart that this was for keeps. In fact she couldn't imagine anything in existence that was powerful enough to pull them apart.

So far Ed had been unable to find another car. He had discussed the matter at great length with both Sharon and Mike, and had decided that another BMW would be his first choice. Conversations with the insurance company had confirmed that a cheque would be with him any day now, but perusal of the local advertising paper had confirmed that he had probably paid over the odds for the red one and was unlikely to receive all his money back. However, the good news was that there seemed to be dozens of BMW's for sale, all in good condition and all at a reasonable price, and Sharon and Ed were really enjoying viewing and driving them all. They seemed to range from the very good to the very bad. Some had clearly been raced, and others had changed hands so many times that they had obviously never been loved.

The ones to look out for had been cherished from new and were simply being replaced by a newer model. Ed had found two such cars, one black and one navy. Neither was a convertible as this seemed to push the price up tremendously, and he had decided that in the long run, a standard hard top was his most sensible option, especially if the future of his garage was in the balance. Sharon liked the black one best but it was a year older and had more miles on the clock. Apart from that there was little to choose between them, and anyway, they could both be sold by the time his cheque came through. Still, it was fun looking.

It was Thursday evening and Ed was just about to leave for a solo gig when his mobile rang. It was Lou Parrott. He didn't need to ask her to be brief because, thankfully, that was her way.

"Hello Ed! Lou here! How are you?"

"I'm fine Lou! And you?"

"Oh, same as usual. Look! I'm ringing to ask you a favour."

"Go on!"

"Well it's more of an invitation really. What are you up to this Saturday lunch time?"

"Nothing that I know of," said Ed. "Why?"

"Well, did you know that Helen is out of hospital."

"No I didn't!" said Ed, walking round the flat with his mobile, gathering his last few things. "That's great news."

"Yes, isn't it," said Lou. "Well she's back home and her parents are putting on a barbeque for her. They want to know if you'll come."

"Yes! I'd love to. Would it be all right if I bring a friend?"

"Of course. We'd be delighted!"

"Thank you," said Ed. "Do you need picking up?"

"No, that's all taken care of. I'm going round in the morning to help with the preparations."

"You'd better give me the time and the address then."

Ed quickly phoned Sharon and told her about Saturday. She was delighted and he arranged to pick her up at midday.

"Are you going out now?" she asked. He told her that he was playing a solo gig tonight.

"Have a good time then." She sounded wistful and on impulse Ed asked if she wanted to come along.

"I'm playing at the Heath Lodge and I have to leave now to give myself time to set up," he said, "but if you get a taxi over I'll pay for it and I'll take you home afterwards."

"Are you sure that's OK?" she asked. "I don't want to get in the way." Ed realized that he'd been a little hard on her before, and if he hadn't invited her this time, she would never have asked.

"No silly!" he said. "I want you to come. Please?"

"OK!" she said, sounding happy again. "I'll come straight over!"

"No need to hurry. I don't start till eight thirty."

The hotel was fairly quiet and Ed didn't actually start till nearly nine o'clock as most of the guests were still having their dinner. He sat at the bar and waited for Sharon to arrive and for once he wasn't wearing his cowboy hat. The guests started to trickle in at ten-to, and Ed was disappointed that Sharon still hadn't arrived. At five-to he got down from his bar stool and picked up his guitar. It took a minute to sort out his leads and when he was ready he looked up and saw Sharon watching from the doorway. He smiled warmly and nodded to her. She sat down at a small table on her own near the bar.

Ed was surprised how nervous it made him feel, just to have someone there that he knew. He introduced himself and started with a version of *'Take the Ribbon from my Hair'*. There was a fairly generous smattering of applause at the end, and Ed noticed that Sharon was clapping, though he couldn't see her face because of the lights. He did a couple more slow numbers, then woke them up a little with '*Rhinestone Cowboy*'. This time the response was more enthusiastic and he tried out a waltz. Two couples got up to dance, and were soon joined by a few more. He went into a Kenny Rogers number as a quickstep and soon the tiny dance floor was almost full and he lost sight of Sharon altogether. After forty five minutes he announced a short break and went over to join her.

After the phone call, Sharon was thrown into a frenzy of activity deciding what to wear. Not that she was exactly spoilt for choice. Eventually she settled on a long black skirt and the blouse that Ed had helped her to choose on that first shopping trip together. She wore a little more make-up than usual and the perfume that she saved for 'best'. Daz was upstairs in his room and she knocked on his door and told him that she was going out. Slowly his door opened and his head poked out. He looked her up and down.

"I suppose you're seeing 'him' again"

"Who?" asked Sharon.

"Ed!"

"Yes, Ed! Why?"

"Because it's bloody stupid, that's why," and he went to slam the door, but Sharon was too quick and put her foot neatly in the gap. She was really angry.

"What the hell is that supposed to mean?"

"It means you're far too old for him. Anyway, you look ridiculous and you smell like a tart!"

"How dare you!" she yelled. "You nasty, spoilt little brat! Why do you have to try and spoil everything I do?"

"Because he was a friend of mine, and now he's your fucking toy boy. How do you suppose that makes me feel?"

"If you gave a damn about anyone else's feelings then I might give that question some serious thought, but as it is I've had it with you and your rudeness."

"And I've had it with you, you old cow!" shouted Daz.

"Good! You can stay alone in your room all evening again. At least someone wants to spend it with me. Get a life Daz, before you start ripping mine to pieces. Goodnight!"

Sharon went downstairs and started to phone for a taxi, but tears began to well up in her eyes and she wished she wasn't going out at all. Daz seemed to be getting worse again, and she didn't know what to do. All her efforts to keep a nice home together for him seemed to go unappreciated, and part of her wanted to throw him out and force him to start making his own way in the world. All the time that she was loving and protecting him he was never going to grow up, but love him she did. That was her little boy. It was her job! Why did it have to be so heartbreaking?

But now she had Ed, and surely it was time to put herself first. If she didn't go tonight then Ed would be worried and Daz would think that he had won. It would be a mistake to let him think he had any power over her. Better to go out and leave him to stew. She had done her best and she could do no more. There was a lovely man out there awaiting her arrival and she would be a fool to let him slip through her fingers for the sake of an angry boy who should know better. Sharon picked up the receiver and dialled the number of the taxi company. While she was waiting she popped into the bathroom and fixed her make-up.

When she finally arrived at the hotel, Ed was only just starting. He saw her come in and smiled warmly at her. Sharon smiled back and self consciously found a seat at an empty table near the back of the room. The whole lounge bar was dated, but it felt cheerful and cosy. Ed started to sing an old country ballad and Sharon found herself almost mesmerised by the smooth warmth of his voice. When the song had finished she found herself clapping enthusiastically, and blushed furiously when she realised that he had noticed. After a couple of songs she went to the bar to get herself a drink, she needed one! The barman had clocked the look between them when she had entered and spoke to her as she approached.

"Are you here with Ed then?" he said.

"Yes, sort of."

"Bloody good, isn't he?" said the barman. "The guests really love him." Sharon glowed with pride, thinking that they weren't the only ones.

"Could I have a dry Martini and lemonade please?"

In the break Ed came over and gave her a peck on the cheek, then sat down on the chair next to hers placing his pint on the table before him.

"Everything OK?" he asked.

"Yes fine! Daz was playing up though when I left. Sorry I was late."

"It's OK. You didn't miss much."

"On the contrary," she said. "Your music is lovely! I could listen to you all night."

"Be careful what you wish for!" said Ed with a laugh. "You might get stuck with me." They went out onto the balcony, away from prying eyes. The bay curved away below them, strung with tiny dotted lights and a gentle breeze ruffled their hair.

"Are you warm enough?" asked Ed, slipping his arms round her.

"I am now," she replied. "It's so lovely up here. You can't tell from the road that this view is here."

"This view," said Ed gazing into her eyes, "is anywhere I want it to be."

"I meant," said Sharon, "Oh never mind!" and they kissed a long deep kiss. When they finally separated Sharon said,

"Hadn't you better get back? Your public is waiting!"

"Spoilsport!" said Ed. They went back into the lounge and Ed moved Sharon to a table nearer to the stage where he could see her all the time and she wouldn't feel so alone. He left her with a smile and sat back on the stool with his guitar. There was a small ripple of applause and then Ed did something he had never done before as he announced his first song.

"Ladies and gentlemen. I would like to dedicate this first song to a very special person who is here tonight. I wrote it myself and I hope you will indulge me for the next four and a half minutes. Thank you."

The room hushed and Ed began to pick out the notes of the sad, pretty tune he had written in his room only a couple of weeks before. He sang earnestly and sometimes with his eyes shut, and as he played and sang he held the room spellbound. Sharon felt the loneliness and despair he must have felt as he wrote it, and listening to him now, she felt her own heart break. Was Daz right? Was she a sad older woman chasing a toy boy? Was she fooling herself? She knew now with certainty that she wanted this man before her more than anything in the world, but couldn't for the life of her see what she had to offer him. Then she noticed that he was looking straight into her eyes and he was singing to her; only to her. There was love and reassurance in those brown eyes, and all her doubts and fears began to melt away. Something very special was happening tonight.

The lunchtime barbeque turned out to be a brilliant success and Ed wouldn't have missed it for the world, but it turned out to be an unlikely herald for a day that was to end in terror, and eventually tragedy. Ed picked up Sharon as arranged and they arrived just after midday. Mary Parrott rushed to meet them both with a big kiss, and then shepherded them eagerly into the back garden where she pressed a drink into their hands.

Helen was there looking lovely in distressed jeans and a pink sun top, her scars almost completely faded or concealed. A group of her friends were lounging around on the grass or leaning on the wall next to her with bottles of alco-pops in their hands. She had pinned up the sides of her long blonde hair and applied a little make-up, and Sharon was amused to see her blush a little as Ed walked in.

"I think I've got competition!" she said in his ear.

"It's all right. I don't fancy young birds," he replied with a grin, then he walked forward and gave Helen a self conscious peck on the cheek in front of all her mates. Helen blushed a deeper shade of pink and a couple of her friends started sniggering, though it was obvious to Sharon that they were envious.

"Helen! You look great!" he said. "How are you?"

"I'm fine thanks!" she said cooly, aware that her friends were watching. "Thanks for coming."

"Thanks for inviting us," he replied. "You won't remember Sharon."

"No I don't. Did you come to the hospital too?"

"Yes I did," said Sharon, shaking her hand warmly. "It's lovely to meet you at last. You look really gorgeous!"

"Thanks," said Helen. "I'll look better when these have gone." She touched the slight ridges which had formed on the damaged side of her face.

"But they hardly notice!"

"Really?"

"Really!" said Sharon and Ed together, and laughed.

"You two make a really good pair, you know." said Helen. Sharon looked at Ed and said

"I know!"

Just then, Ed was pleased to see Dave walk in with a young lady in tow, and for a moment he thought it was the WPC he had met before, but as they approached he realized he was mistaken. They shook hands and then introduced the girls to each other. Ed was amazed to see that Dave had brought Janice, the nurse from the hospital. That must have been fast work! Sharon took Janice off to find drinks while the boys caught up.

"How's it going with the car?" asked Dave.

"I've borrowed one for now," said Ed, "but I'm looking out for another BMW."

"Are the insurance going to pay up?"

"It looks like it. How long have you known Janice then?"

"About half an hour, actually. We were both invited, and Helen's Aunty Lou asked if I would mind picking her up."

"Oh!" said Ed. "I'm sorry! I assumed you were together."

"Give me another half hour and you never know. Apparently she's single." Ed had to smile. Louisa Potts was meddling again.

"Any news on the case?"

"Not really," replied Dave. "You know I hate this bit, waiting for him to make his next move, and knowing that someone will probably get hurt in the process. Look at her!" he said nodding at Helen. "She's one of the lucky ones, and who knows what damage she has really suffered. Even little Kelly Foster is still having nightmares!" Dave spoke with a passion and conviction that Ed found moving.

"Watch out," he said. "The girls are coming back."

"Don't get Janice on the subject for God's sake," said Dave. "What she'd like to do to him isn't something you'd want to discuss in polite company. It made my eyes water I can tell you!" The girls wandered over and Janice put a drink in Dave's hand. He thanked her and they retained eye contact for a moment longer than was strictly necessary. 'Good old Lou!' thought Ed.

The delicious smell of cooking meat was wafting over and Ed wondered how soon he could decently go in search of lunch. Dennis Parrott appeared to be hopefully poking something on the barbeque while Mary kept arriving with bowls of salad and baps.

"Oh my God!" said Dave suddenly. "Don't look now. It's the spectre at the feast!" Ed looked round and saw Danny White loitering hopefully by the gate. Helen appeared by her mother.

"What did you invite him for?" she hissed.

"I didn't dear!" she replied. "Well aren't you going to invite him in. I thought you two were friends."

"Do me a favour!" moaned Helen dramatically, before waving a limp hand in Danny's direction. Needing no further encouragement, Danny marched in, grinning round at everybody. The kids in the corner started giggling again, and Ed noticed that one or two were holding their noses; obviously some sort of private joke. Dave was surprised to see him there, especially as his father was in a lot of trouble right now. Also, considering Arnie White's opinion of Helen, it was probable that he didn't even know that Danny was here. Mary gave Danny a glass of cola and encouraged him to go and join Helen and his 'friends'.

"Hello Helen," he said. "It's nice to see you back."

"Thanks," she replied, then turned back to her mates. Danny leant against the wall on his own nearby and sipped his cola, without taking his eyes off her. She began to feel fidgety and wished with all her heart that he hadn't come. He was giving her the creeps.

The food was finally ready and Mary gave them all a paper plate and made them queue in an orderly fashion. Ed was amused to see that the plates were pink and patterned with balloons like the kind you see at kids parties. There were sausages, burgers and some small steaks, and it was all delicious. Sharon and Janice were getting on famously and were arranging for the four of them to meet up for a night out. The wine had been flowing freely and they were quite giggly. The teenagers were getting a bit loud on their alco-pops, and someone had gone off to get a guitar, and was now yelling an almost unrecognisable pop song.

"Go on Ed," urged Sharon. "Show them how it's done."

"Shut up!" replied Ed. "Don't you dare."

"Ooh touchy! Why not?" she asked.

"I just don't want to. This party isn't about me."

"You just don't want to show them up."

"Well it wouldn't be difficult now, would it?" he replied.

The party was winding down at last, and the first few people were beginning to leave when Dave and Ed were suddenly aware of a disturbance in the corner. Danny white was shaking with rage, and the guy who had been playing the guitar was standing with his arm round Helen and grinning at him, clearly winding him up.

"Throw him in the fishpond!" someone shouted. "He might smell better."

"What about it Danny Boy?" he said. "Can't you swim?"

"Better not," someone else jeered. "We don't want to poison the fish!"

"You bastards!" said Danny.

"Don't worry," said the lad. "Helen might give you the kiss of life. You'd like that wouldn't you?"

"Leave it out, Rob!" said Helen. Rob was grinning at his mates as Dave and Ed walked over to break it up, so he never saw it coming.

Danny suddenly launched himself at Rob, knocking him to the ground, and started to strangle him. Dave and Ed were on him in a trice and pulling him off, but he wouldn't let go. They had a shoulder each and were dragging him upwards, but his hands stayed firmly round Rob's neck, and then the gagging, choking noises stopped as Rob started to go limp.

"I'll have to hit him!" said Dave.

"Allow me!" replied Ed, and aimed a punch at the side of Danny's head. Instantly he loosened his grip as his head snapped sideways, and they managed to drag him off. Rob was a dreadful shade of grey but at least he was breathing. Helen was sobbing and her friends were almost hysterical. Danny rolled over and got onto his feet.

"I'm going to get you all you bastards," he said, swaying slightly. "Just you wait!" and he ran out of the garden and off up the road before anyone could stop him.

"And I said he didn't have it in him!" said Dave.

"What?" said Ed, kneeling down beside the wheezing Rob.

"Oh nothing," said Dave. "Why did you hit him?"

"Because you're a copper. You could have lost your job."

"Thanks mate! I owe you one."

Quite a crowd had gathered and Dave took out his warrant card and held it up as Janice took a look at Rob.

"It's OK everyone, the show's over," he said. "It's just kids who've had much too drink." He looked down at Janice and she nodded.

"He's fine!" she said. Secretly she thought the little sod deserved it. Ed asked Sharon if she was ready to go home.

"Yes please," she said gratefully. Dave looked at Janice.

"Are you ready, too?" She smiled and nodded. They went and said their goodbyes to Dennis and Mary, who thankfully had been clearing up through most of the fuss. Then they all kissed Helen goodbye and promised to keep in touch.

"I'm sorry it was spoilt," said Helen, sadly.

"That's OK!" said Sharon brightly. "A party's not a party without a good fight at the end!"

On the way out, Ed said to Dave,

"What did you mean when you said that you didn't think he had it in him?"

"Oh nothing," said Dave.

"You think it's him, don't you?"

"Truthfully, no. But he fit's the description, he has a motive of sorts, and he *was* there!"

Chapter 16

Ed had a private gig that night with Mike, but there was time for a cup of coffee at Sharon's before he left. Driving her home, he wished he could take her with him but it just wasn't practical. She wouldn't be allowed in the ballroom, and she couldn't spend most of the evening on her own in the hotel bar. Even so, they could hardly bare to be parted for a minute these days, and Ed couldn't help but wonder about their future together. It was almost inconceivable that they should spend it apart. For a moment he ran through this wild imaginary phone call in his head.

"Hi Mum. Hi Dad. Great news! I'm moving into a council house with a single mum called Sharon!"

She saw him grin and wondered what was up but he didn't think that she would see the funny side just yet.

"Did you have a good time?" he asked instead.

"Yes, it was lovely, except for the end."

"I know. That was a shame, especially for Helen," he said. "I'm sure that Danny wasn't even invited."

"He's obviously got a huge thing about her."

"Well she is a terrible flirt. Did you know that she's come on to both me and Dave?"

"I kind of guessed. Do you think she might have encouraged Danny at some point then?" she asked.

"I think it's entirely possible. He does wear trousers."

"Oh! Then I'd better put you in a skirt!"

They got to Sharon's and chatted in the kitchen while she filled the kettle and sorted out the mugs. She reached up into a cupboard for the jar of coffee and Ed grabbed her round the waist. She shrieked.

"I nearly dropped the coffee, you idiot."

"Well turn round and I'll give you something even better." Laughing, she wriggled round in his arms and his lips found hers. Suddenly a noise in the hall made them break apart, and they looked up and saw Daz glaring at them.

"Sorry Daz!" said Sharon, trying not to laugh. "I didn't hear you come down!"

Although it was fairly dark in the hall so they couldn't see his face, Ed realized that Daz was swaying slightly on his feet.

"Whore!" he said to his mother. Sharon grabbed Ed's arm tightly.

"Just leave it," she said urgently. "He sometimes gets like this!" But Ed was having none of it.

"How dare you, you little bastard!" he shouted, ripping his arm free and walking into the hall. Daz was wearing his filthy old coat, and his face was sweating and his eyes were sort of glazed. Instantly Ed knew what was going on.

"What have you taken?" he yelled. "Where are they?" He grabbed Daz by the lapels of his coat and shook him.

"Get off me you mother-fucker!" slurred Daz. Ed couldn't believe his ears, even though he had the sense to realize that Daz was off his head on something.

"You promised me!" Ed shouted in his face." You promised you'd get off the junk and look after your mum. Now where is it?" He tore at the pockets of Daz's coat. "Is it in here?" Daz tried to fight him off but his blows were confused and ineffectual. Sharon just stood behind in shock. Ed's hand closed round a tobacco tin in the inside pocket and he pulled it free and took off the lid. Inside was a small cellophane packet containing a fair quantity of white powder and a used syringe.

"Where did you get this?" he asked. Daz didn't answer.

"Where?" shouted Ed again. "Have you been seeing Les again?" This time Daz looked up and Ed knew that he had struck a note. "Oh for fuck's sake Daz! Why?"

Sharon came up behind him and said,

"What's going on? What's Les got to do with anything?" Ed looked round at her stricken face and suddenly Daz took his opportunity and tore himself free. As he bolted, Ed grabbed at the hem of his coat and there was a ripping sound. Something hard fell to the floor and quick as a flash Ed picked it up.

"What's this?" asked Ed. Daz froze in his tracks. He turned. Ed was holding a penknife; a burgundy army style penknife with lots of blades and a small white cross and circle emblem on the side.

"Give it back," said Daz, his voice suddenly calm. "It's mine." Ed continued to stare at the knife, realization slowly dawning.

"Mum?" pleaded Daz urgently.

"Give it him back," said Sharon. "It was his Dad's." Slowly, Ed held out the knife, knowing that he was making a mistake yet unable to resist, and as Daz reached out and took it their eyes met. Ed knew, and Daz knew that Ed knew. Somehow the tin had ended up on the floor and Daz calmly picked it up and walked swiftly but slightly unsteadily out of the house.

For a moment there was silence then Sharon exploded, demanding that Ed tell her everything. There were tears in her eyes and panic in her voice. Ed lead her firmly into the lounge and sat her down in the armchair while he perched on the sofa, dreading the ordeal that lay ahead.

"Tell me everything! Now Ed!"

"OK," he said. "Just try and bare in mind that I was trying to protect you."

"I want to know about my son!" she persisted. So poor Ed had to tell her everything; from the deal Daz had with Les to the argument on the beach, and as he talked he could see her pain and disbelief building but she kept on asking him questions, especially about Les.

"Poor Daz!" she said. "If only I'd known what he was going through."

"But did you never suspect?" asked Ed. "You said yourself that Les had some dodgy friends."

"Do you really think I would have kept him around if I had?" Ed didn't answer. There was nothing he could say to soften the blows. She had the facts now and she would have to work through them as best she could, while he still had to figure out the significance of the knife. Sadly he knew that nothing would ever be the same for the two of them again.

"I'm sorry!" said Ed.

"Sorry?" she shouted. "Bloody sorry? How the hell could you keep a thing like this from me? There was me thinking that you were the greatest thing since sliced bread and all the time you've been keeping secrets from me. Christ I've been such a fool. Why the hell didn't you tell me?"

"Because Daz made me promise that I wouldn't."

"Daz doesn't know what bloody day it is. I'm his mother! I've got a right to know. I trusted you."

"Well just you shout at me if it makes you feel better," said Ed angrily. "I'm not the one who brought a drug dealer into my house! How could you be so bloody stupid?"

"Get out!" she screamed. "Go on, get out!"

Sadly Ed rose and headed for the door. There really was nothing left to say. He was damned if he was going to take the blame for this, and he had to get back now anyway if he didn't want to be late for Mike.

When Ed reached the flat he sent Sharon a text on his mobile. It simply said "Is it over?" A minute later he received her reply. "Yes. Sorry." Despite feeling like he wanted to die, Ed prepared to put on a brave face and do what he did best. Mike picked up on his mood and asked him if he was OK.

"Yes, I'm fine," he said. "It's just that Sharon and me are finished."

"Oh! Do you want to talk about it?"

"I don't really know what I want," said Ed.

"Wasn't it working out then?"

"On the contrary, it was working out fine! It was just her teenage son."

"Seems a bloody silly reason to break up to me!" said Mike, and they left it at that.

That evening passed for Ed in a bit of a blur. He couldn't have done too badly because they got a great round of applause at the end, and Mike even took another booking. They had a quiet pint together at the end while the staff were removing the dance floor, which fitted over the carpet in sections, but no more was said about Sharon. Instead Mike chatted about the kids, in particular the impending birthday party, but he could see that none of it was sinking in. He was sorry to think that Ed would be on his own again, and prayed that Trish wouldn't carry out her threat to set him up with one of her single mates.

On his way home, Ed realized that he hadn't eaten since the barbeque, and drove to the kebab shop. Without thinking, he took the steaming package up to the top car park to eat and to think. It was a still night and he could just make out the lights of the town, twinkling between the branches of the trees. Despite his heavy heart, the kebab tasted great, and although there was far too much chilli sauce on it for his taste, for some reason the burn felt good. Like when he split up with Lisa, his emotions seemed to be turned off, and once again he felt like he was running on empty, just going through the motions. He wondered why he didn't break down and cry, or take to his bed as others might; it was certainly what he felt like doing, and no-one would stop him, but he remembered Lou telling him that he had a lot of inner strength, and just maybe it was true. He was feeling sorry for himself but it would pass. It would have to. He considered the idea of going back to Sharon, of begging for a second chance, but too much had been said and he knew that, like the last time, there was no going back.

Suddenly there was a high pitched scream from the trees on his right, near the graveyard path. It was definitely a woman's scream, and there seemed to be no-one else around. Ed couldn't believe it. This was a nightmare. He got out of the car, just as there was another cry, fairly close this time. Someone was definitely in trouble. Feeling as though he were in a bad dream, Ed ran across the car park and down the narrow path, cursing that he hadn't got a torch this time. The dim orange glow of the lamps was enough to see by so long as he stayed on the path. He called out. There was nothing.

He slowed to a walk and looked around carefully, aware that he was alone and comforted by the weight of the mobile phone in his pocket. As he drew level with the tomb where Lou had been digging about he noticed something small and brown on the ground, right in the middle of the path. At first it looked like a large, flat, dead leaf, but as he approached it turned out to be a wallet, a brown, square wallet with a round motif in the middle. How strange. Ed bent down to pick it up, and as he did so, something struck a chord in his memory. In a flash he saw a scrap of white paper with a picture of a square with a circle in the centre, exactly the same shape and size as what he was seeing now. His heart missed a beat and his blood ran cold.

Dave was sat in the centre of Bournemouth with Sam Wallis in the squad car again. It had been a busy night in town, with several skirmishes breaking out as the clubs emptied, but thankfully there had been no arrests, so no extra paperwork. They had chatted for a bit but had now had lapsed into silence as Dave replayed in his mind the conversation he had had earlier. He received a message that someone was asking for him at the front desk, just after he had come on his shift, and was surprised to find Sharon, looking very upset. He had taken her through to the interview room and had made her a coffee.

The tale she had to tell him was incredible, and although she admitted that she had been very stupid, his heart went out to her. She was also worried sick about her son, and asked if he would help find him as she was afraid he would do something stupid. Dave immediately got a message down to the control room for all units to be on the lookout, and gave out the description of Daz. When Sharon left, he almost called Ed but decided against it. Things had obviously gone badly wrong between those two and he was genuinely sorry. Besides, she had given him enough information to be going on with for the moment.

He pulled up the file on Lesley Andrew Baker, and was pleased to see that he had a record as long as his arm. He had been convicted of drug dealing and supplying, and had even had a couple of spells in prison, but so far it had all been for fairly small amounts. There was also a conviction for receiving stolen goods and a GBH thrown in for good measure. All in all he was a fairly typical, all round scum-bag, and it beggared belief that a girl like Sharon had got involved with him in the first place. However, the photo on the file didn't seem to fit the description. He looked clean cut and fairly handsome, and maybe he was a good actor too. If he drove a nice car, wore smart clothes and was an accomplished liar, how was a girl supposed to know? Dave rubbed his hands together and took the file up to show Mercier, and was pleased to learn that, until recently, Baker had been under observation. Well, they had enough to nail the bastard properly now!

Ed cautiously picked up the wallet and hurried back to the car, then he got out his mobile and pressed Dave's number. Suddenly there was a rustle on the back seat behind him and a sharp pain in the back of his neck. He froze.

"Put that down!" said a familiar voice. Ed closed his phone and dropped it on the seat next to him.

"Hello Daz," he said, a lot more calmly than he felt. "I was wondering when you would show up again."

"I knew you would work it out sooner or later," said Daz. "Why did you have to spoil everything?" Ed's mind was racing. There was nothing he could do to help himself. The best thing would be to keep Daz talking.

"Who was that screaming?" asked Ed.

"It was me," said Daz. "Did I fool you?"

"Yes, you sure did. It sounded just like a woman."

"Well I've heard enough women screaming lately to know what one sounds like," said Daz with a laugh. "Did you find my wallet?"

"Oh yes. Here it is."

"Don't turn round," said Daz sharply.

"OK, OK," said Ed, and he tossed it over to the back seat. "So what happens now?"

"Well, the thing is, you're the only one who knows what I've done," said Daz. "And it's such a shame, because I really liked you. Really!"

"And I like you Daz, a lot, but I don't understand why you did things to those girls?"

"Because they were asking for it!"

"Yeah?" said Ed, playing along. "I guess I know what you mean. So what did they do to you?" (Keep him talking, keep him talking). Daz stayed silent for a few moments, then, just as Ed was about to ask again, he started.

"I had a girlfriend," said Daz. "She let me buy her drinks and stuff, and she wore these little itsy bitsy skirts so that I could practically see her knickers."

"She sounds nice." (Keep him talking).

"She looked alright but she was a real bitch. She got me all wound up so I didn't know what I was doing. She even let me kiss her, but when I wanted more, she wouldn't let me. She let me see it all but then she made a real bad fuss. Next time I saw her she was with her mates and they were all laughing at me."

"What a bitch," said Ed sympathetically.

"Yeah, I reckon so too! So I decided to help myself. It's quite simple really. You see, no-one laughs at me."

"But you didn't know any of those girls, did you?"

"No!" said Daz, "But they're all the same you know. I only picked the ones who were asking for it. Why do they wear that stuff, man?"

"You tell me?"

"Because they want us to look at them! They want to offer it on a plate, then take it away. Well not me. If it's on offer, then I'm having some, even if I have to help myself."

"Sounds reasonable to me," said Ed, struggling for something to say. "Do you want to tell me what happened."

"Why should I?"

"Because I really want to know. What does it feel like? It must be great! The excitement, the power!"

"OK. I wanted you to understand," said Daz, "but afterwards you know you have to die, don't you."

"Yeah. I know."

Sharon sat on the sofa, staring into the mug of tea that she made an hour ago but hadn't touched. It was nearly two thirty on Sunday morning and her life lay in ruins. She wondered where Ed was and what he was doing, probably tucked up in bed by now. She wondered what Daz was up to, and where he would be spending the night. How much of this had been her fault? Ed had been the best thing to happen to her in years, but as in all things, maybe it really had been too good to be true. For a single bloke like Ed, there would always be another woman; younger, prettier. For now she would have to dedicate her life to sorting out her son. It was partly her who had got him into this mess by bringing Les into their lives, so she surely owed him that much. It was obvious now that while she had Daz on her hands, she could never have a proper relationship with any man. There was no point even bothering to try any more.

Daz continued to press the knife into Ed's neck, but now he launched into his sickening story, eager to share the details that had been his secret for so long.

"The first one was a mistake. She was stronger than she looked and she got away. It was my own fault. I should have been ready. I had the knife in my pocket but I didn't get it out. That's why I had to run away. She gave me a cracking black eye."

"So when you disappeared, it was to hide your black eye?" said Ed. "You didn't want anyone to put two and two together. Where did you go?"

"Like I told you, I stayed in a squat in Southampton till the bruise had almost gone, but the guys in there were really bad and it was dirty and smelly. They were stealing off me so I left as soon as I could."

"Then what?" urged Ed. (Keep him talking, wait your chance.)

"I got the train back to Bournemouth station and walked into town. That's when I got that blonde bird. I couldn't believe it. She was beautiful, and mine for the taking. I was really going to enjoy teaching her a lesson, but then along *you* came and spoilt it. I wanted to kill you then."

"I'm sorry," said Ed. "I didn't know. But why did you have to hurt her so badly?"

"I had to shut her up or you would have seen us."

"Yeah! I suppose so." Ed was sickened as the image of poor Helen came back to him. He fought to keep his voice under control. "So what about the last one? Why did you kill her?"

"Now that wasn't my fault! I never meant to kill her. I met her in Bournemouth. She told me her name was Claudia and she was from Spain."

"Go on!"

"I saw her trying to light her fag but her lighter wouldn't work. I lit it for her with a match." Daz gave a queer little laugh. "It was like a scene from one of those movies. There was this queue of people all waiting for taxis and she was on her own at the back. She was wearing tight jeans and a white top. She looked quite nice but she was really stupid. Honest to God, I didn't plan that one, it just sort of happened! We got talking and I offered her a lift home in my car. I couldn't believe it when she came with me. I think she might even have gone with me, but when we got to the park I tried to kiss her and she started shouting at me in Spanish."

"Then what happened," said Ed.

"I got out the knife to shut her up, but she started screaming. She just went mad. I put it away to see if she would stop but she just carried on. She didn't even try and run away, she just screamed, so I took out the knife and I stabbed her. Funny thing is I don't remember actually doing it." Ed realized that the pressure of the point on his neck was lessening now. Just keep him talking.

"That's a shame. I would really like to know what it feels like."

"Would you? Would you really?" Daz sounded pleased. Then he surprised Ed "Your woman dumped on you didn't she?"

"Yes," said Ed. "Who told you?"

"No-one told me. I was there.......!"

"What do you mean, you were there?"

"She was up here, in this car park!" This was new territory and Ed wondered where he was leading.

"Go on," he said.

"I come up here quite a lot. There's a place in the cemetery where you can sleep and nobody bothers you. I like to come here at night and watch what people get up to in their cars. Well one night, it must be over a year ago now, there was this couple having it away in this red car. The whole car was swaying so I knew they were at it. I got right up close to the window and they didn't know I was there. She had lovely creamy skin and dark hair, and he was blonde. I think it was your wife."

"Why?"

"Because I saw her a couple of months later coming out of the cinema and she was with you. I'm real good with faces. I recognised you straight away when you started hanging around here and I guessed what had happened. Later on Mum told me you had been dumped by your wife. Was that her?"

"Yes, that was her," said Ed. He was feeling sick. Enough was enough. He had to get out.

"She was lovely. I can't think what you see in my mum." Another thought occurred to Ed.

"Did you set fire to my car?"

"Yes. Sorry about that!"

"But why?"

"Because you lied to me. You said there was nothing going on!" the pressure on the blade had increased again, and Ed felt what was probably blood dripping down the side of his neck.

"I wasn't lying Daz. That night I was playing in a band at a party. I didn't know your mum was going to be there."

"So? You didn't have to pull her!"

"I didn't. Les dumped her at the party. I couldn't leave her there. It was the middle of the forest and it was raining," said Ed. "Anyway, what were you doing at my place?"

"I needed to talk to you. I couldn't go home in case Les was there, and it was too cold to sleep out. I didn't think you'd mind if I stayed at your place but your car wasn't there so I waited. Then you turned up with my mum. I was so angry. You promised!" Ed could see it all now. The answers were fitting together.

"I'm sorry," said Ed. "That must have looked bad." Since they had been in the car together, Ed realized that Daz had started to slur his words slightly, also that the tip of the blade against his neck had begun to quiver.

"Yeah man, real bad." (Oh God! Change the subject. Keep him talking.)

"So when you hurt those girls, what exactly did you want out of it?"

"I wanted sex. I've never actually done it."

"Oh!"

"I was going to make them do it with me. I wanted to know what it felt like."

"You were going to rape them?"

"S'pose so, but when I got there it wasn't that easy. I didn't really know how, and something always went wrong!"

"So you still haven't, you know, done it?" If it hadn't been so tragic, Ed would have felt like laughing. What an awful, pitiful mess!

"Next time," said Daz, "I'll get it right. They won't keep getting away with it." His speech was getting slower. Ed saw a sliver of hope, and grasped at it.

"Daz? Have you taken something?"

"Oh man! Don't start giving me that shit again. Anyway, why should you care?" Ed carried on.

"I don't really. I just wondered if you've got any stuff on you?"

"Why?"

"Are you really going to kill me?" asked Ed.

"Don't want to but I got to!" Daz's speech was slowing even more.

"Can I have some? Please Daz?"

"What for?"

"'Cause it's ages since I had any. We used to have it all the time as kids."

"Get away!" said Daz.

"No! Think about it. We lived in a village, miles from anywhere, and to be honest there was nothing else to do. So, this one guy, Steve, he used to go down to Bournemouth on his bike and come back with a load of stuff. We used to give him all our pocket money."

"No shit!"

Ed laughed. "Our parents would have killed us, but we hid in this barn and we never got caught. We used to get a load of beers in and had a brill time. We did some really stupid things."

"How old were you?"

"I dunno. About fifteen I guess. My mates were older." Ed felt Daz begin to relax, and as they talked he slowly moved his hand, inch by inch, till it was resting on the door handle.

"It sounds great," said Daz.

"It was," said Ed. "Go on! Give me some! What have you got? Cocaine? H?"

"H! It's real pure stuff. You'll only need a little."

"Great! Please Daz. Call it my last request. Anyway, if you are going to kill me, I might not mind so much if I'm stoned." Ed's hand grasped the handle as he pleaded, careful not to tense his shoulder in case Daz should notice, fighting to keep his breath normal.

"OK!" said Daz finally. "Can't see why not."

The point of the blade stayed in place while he removed the tin from his pocket, then Ed heard the slight metallic click as the lid came off. Quick as a flash, Ed yanked the door handle and shot out of the car. Daz let out an angry yell behind him, as Ed's legs carried him as fast as they could across the car park to the top of the steps. He risked a quick look back and found that Daz had given pursuit, but his strides were uneven and he was a long way back. Ed escaped down the steps and ran into town.

Chapter 17

Ed walked through the dark streets of Bournemouth, cursing that he'd had to leave his mobile phone behind. For the first time in days, light drops of rain began to fall making halos around the street lamps, and the roads and pavements were slick and reflective. Ed didn't mind the rain. He had never felt so miserable in all his life, and a walk in the rain at three o'clock in the morning felt like as good a way as any to pass the time.

Where could he go? He couldn't go home. Someone out there was trying to kill him. He should go straight to the police station, but the thought of being shut up in a small room with Mercier right now was unbearable. If only he had his mobile he could get straight through to Dave, but without it he didn't know the number. He felt the wetness seeping through his clothes to his shoulders and realized that he was still wearing his dinner suit. Eventually he made a decision and flagged down a passing taxi. The driver looked a little surprised at his appearance but had too much experience under his belt to pass comment.

Mike was sat up watching the end of a film that Trish had thoughtfully recorded for him earlier that night. Sometimes after a gig he knew that sleep wouldn't come and he was far more comfortable on the sofa in front of the telly than trying to lie still and not disturb his wife. Part of the reason he couldn't settle tonight was Ed. He knew that a lot of bad stuff was happening in Ed's life right now, but that still didn't account for the uneasy feeling he was left with. Mike was also painfully aware that, apart from him and Trish, Ed truly had nobody. He realized he'd come to look on Ed almost like a younger brother, though he'd never actually had one of his own. He hoped that if Ed ever needed help, he would feel he could turn to them. It was while he was having these thoughts that he heard a taxi pull up, and then a soft tapping on his window.

Therefore it wasn't much of a surprise, almost a relief in fact, when he pulled back the curtain and saw Ed's face looking in at him. Mike quietly let him in the front door, and silently took in Ed's appearance. His dinner suit was soaked through and there was what looked like blood on his high shirt collar, dark at the top and faded out into shades of light brown across his chest in the rain soaked cotton.

Ed was relieved that Mike didn't turn a hair at his unexpected arrival. Good old Mike! It was almost as though he had been expecting him.

"Come on in," said Mike. "I was just going to make a coffee."

"Thanks!" said Ed. "I didn't know where else to go."

"Ed. Tell me to mind my own business if you want, but are you in any trouble."

"Depends what you mean. I can't go home. There's someone after me."

"Not the teenage son?" asked Mike in surprise. Ed could have laughed.

"You got it!"

They sat watching the film in silence together, drinking their coffee. It tasted so good. Then he asked Mike if he could use the phone. Mike handed over his mobile as the land line was in the hall and he didn't want to risk waking the family. Ed got through to Bournemouth police station and asked if Dave Walker was on duty. He was told that Dave was out in the squad car, but was due back any minute. Would he like to leave a message? Ed said it was urgent that he call him back on this mobile number immediately. The controller said that she would pass it on.

Dave Walker parked his squad car at the back of the station and took his mobile phone out of the glove box where it had stayed throughout his shift. He was surprised to see that he had a missed call. Sam Wallis was beside him.

"Did you hear my phone go off?"

"No," said Sam. "What time?"

"Just over an hour ago."

"Nope, sorry mate. Anyone important?" He saw it was Ed.

"Could be," replied Dave. "No matter." He pressed the button to call Ed back. The phone rang and he waited for him to answer. The phone rang and rang till he got the message that the person he had called had not responded, and he was cut off. Dave waited for the line to clear, then dialled again.

"Wake up Ed," he said under his breath. The phone rang five times, then suddenly stopped. Dave tried again. Ed's phone had been switched off. Now Dave was feeling uneasy. This didn't make sense. Sam was getting out of the car, and Dave was about to join him when the message came over the radio. He asked the despatcher to wait while he came in. Dave ran to the control room and took the number that Ed had left, then went to his own desk to make the call.

At Mike's house, the mobile sprang to life.

"That was quick," said Ed, practically pouncing on it.

"Hello. Dave?"

"Ed. What's up?"

"I know who it is!" said Ed.

"What are you talking about?"

"The attacks! I know who did them."

"Who?"

"It's Sharon's son. Daz. Darius Court!"

"Are you sure?"

"Yes!" said Ed. "Quite sure! He just held me at knife-point

and confessed."

"Are you OK?"

"Yes, I'm fine. He's out of his head on drugs. I managed to get away."

"Where is he now? We're already searching for him."

"How come?" asked Ed.

"Didn't you know?" asked Dave. "Sharon came to see me yesterday afternoon. She told me all about her boyfriend, Les Baker. Nice bloke!"

"Did she?" asked Ed, amazed. "What about Daz?"

"She was worried sick about him. I promised I'd look out for him so I put a message out to all the cars."

"Well it's him. Last time I saw him he was wandering about in the top car park." A thought occurred to Dave.

"Has he got your mobile phone?"

"Yes. Possibly. I had to leave it."

"Where are you now?"

"I'd rather not say," said Ed. "I can't face being brought in tonight."

"Fair enough," said Dave, "but stay on this number." He rang off.

Ed hadn't realized that Mike had left the room, but he was just walking back in with an armful of blankets and a clean T-shirt. Even so, he had overheard most of the conversation.

"Are you sure you're OK now?" asked Mike. "If there's anything you want to tell me…."

"Thanks but I'm fine. Just a bit tired."

"Well, you get some sleep then. You've done everything you can. We'll talk in the morning. Goodnight!"

"Thanks Mike," said Ed. "Goodnight." Ed started to arrange the blankets on the sofa, and didn't notice Mike pick up the mobile and switch it off. No matter what the world outside was up to, Ed needed nothing more right now than a good night's sleep.

Despite the night's drama, Ed nodded off almost as soon as

his head touched the pillow. Typically for Ed, his last thoughts weren't for himself but for poor old Sharon. Similarly for Mike, now that he knew that Ed was safe, he could sleep soundly too. Funny how he knew that Ed was in danger. Spooky that!

The next morning, Ed woke at about six after a nightmare in which he was being chased through a dark churchyard full of tombs and graves. It was one of those dreams where you can't see what's chasing you, but you have to keep on going. He opened his eyes suddenly and couldn't remember where he was, but for some reason he knew already that it was going to be a bad day. He sat up and rubbed his eyes as the dreadful truth came back to him. He got up and paced round the room. He wished he could put the television on for company but was scared to wake the others.

The first glimmers of daylight were peeping through the curtains and a fine grey drizzle was still falling. What he wanted more than anything right now was to run. He had a sudden urge to be on his own, pounding along the beach, just him and the wind, the rain and the sea. After that, he could maybe face the awful day that undoubtedly lay ahead. Damn! He was miles from home and he didn't have a car. He also felt very uneasy as he remembered that it was the Patel's pride and joy that he had abandoned in the car park. His eyes fixed on Mikes phone on the arm of the sofa and Ed picked it up and switched it on. There were four missed calls. He could deal with those later. Making a sudden decision, Ed dialled the number for a local taxi, and then searched around for a pen and some paper. He left Mike and Trish a note that he had gone for a run and would be back soon for breakfast. He slipped the note under the mobile, neatly folded the blankets and quietly let himself out of the front door wearing the T-shirt and dinner suit.

The taxi driver dropped him off in the car park next to the blue Nova, which unsurprisingly was the only car there. As the taxi drove away he suddenly felt very vulnerable and wished he had asked him to wait while he checked the car. Cautiously he peered in the back window to make sure there was no-one waiting for him in the back. He even checked the boot, his imagination running riot. Although he still had the keys in his pocket and the car had been left unlocked, fortunately it appeared quite unharmed after it's night in the open. Only his phone had disappeared. Ed got in and quickly drove down the slope and away from the car park. After all that had happened to him the previous night, he would be quite happy if he never saw the place again. He went straight to his flat and, keeping a cautious look out, he crept upstairs and changed into his running things, then got back in the car and drove to the cliff top.

It was completely light now and there was a sharp little wind blowing, but the rain had eased off leaving the air damp and murky. Everything looked grey; the sea, the sky. Even the sand seemed drained of colour. Ed shivered and started to run down the zig-zag towards the pier. The fresh air and sudden exertion felt good, and once he was on the flat, he didn't just run, he sprinted. For a few crazy moments he felt that if he ran fast enough, he could leave all his cares behind. The crashing of the waves and the biting wind lifted his spirits and he sped on, almost unaware of the little group of people gathered on the sand on the far side of the pier. As he drew level he noticed a few police uniforms in the group and slowed down, then he spotted Dave.

A cold feeling of dread seized him, though he wasn't quite sure why. Half of him wanted to run on past but Dave had already spotted him and was waving his arms frantically and calling out his name. As he walked over the sand he saw what all the fuss was about, a small, dark bundle huddled on the shoreline. Dave was running towards him, shouting,

"Where the hell have you been? I've been calling you for hours!"

"What's that?" asked Ed, nodding at the bundle.

"You'd better have a look now you're here. You might be

able to identify him." Ed walked over to the body which had been rolled onto it's back. Despite the sickly grey colour there was no mistaking the angular face with the chipped front tooth.

"That's Daz," said Ed quietly.

"You're quite sure?" said Dave.

"Yep!"

"OK. Thanks. We've already contacted the mother and she's on her way over to make the identification."

"Right!" said Ed, not sure what else to say.

"You know you'll have to come in and tell us everything now, don't you?"

"Yes. I'm ready."

"Good."

"Do you know what happened here?" asked Ed.

"We think so," said Dave. "Do me a favour. Go and wait on the steps. I'll be over in a minute." Ed walked back up the beach towards the promenade and sat down on the steps with his head in his hands. What a God-awful mess. Sharon would be here in a minute too. He didn't know how he would handle that. Poor Sharon. He could feel tears stinging the back of his eyes, and looked up to see Dave walking towards him with a blanket, and realized suddenly that he was shivering with the cold. Dave grinned down at him and held out, of all things, a small pewter hip flask.

"Are you alright mate?" he asked, throwing the blanket over Ed's shoulders. "You look done in!" Ed took the flask and had a swig. It was whiskey. He handed it back. "Have another," said Dave sitting down next to him. Ed took another and felt the warmth begin to seep into his bones.

He snuggled thankfully into the scratchy blanket.

"Thanks! Do you know what happened yet?" he asked again.

"A dog walker phoned us just after six to say he'd found a body. He went home just after we got here. A doctor has examined him and although we can't be sure yet, it looks like he either drowned or died of a massive overdose. If you ask me, it's a bit of both. It seems that he meant to take his own life because we think he jumped off the end of the pier, but a couple of officers are over there checking it right now."

"Right!"

"I know it's awful Ed, but at least it's over now."

"I suppose so," replied Ed.

"I know you've been through a lot but once you've given your statement, that should be the end of it."

"I know."

"How about meeting up for that drink soon," said Dave. "I think we've earned it!"

"That sounds good. Thanks mate."

"Hang on a minute," said Dave. "Someone's coming." He got up and walked over to the police car that had pulled up on the promenade, leaving Ed huddled into his blanket on the steps.

The car doors opened and a WPC got out one side and Sharon got out the other. She was wearing jeans and a huge baggy jumper, what looked like slippers and no make-up. She walked across the sand with the WPC on one side and Dave on the other. He watched her small figure in it's huge jumper and wished he could go to her, but he knew that it wasn't his place. A cover had been thrown over the body and Dave stepped forward and lifted it. Ed heard the scream as Sharon looked on the face of her dead son and he saw her fall to the ground. It was too much! Ed had thrown off the blanket and was sprinting over the sand before he even knew what he was doing. He dropped to his knees and gathered Sharon in his arms, holding her tight to him.

"It's alright. I'm here Sharon. I'm here." Her shocked face looked up at him for a moment.

"Oh Ed! Oh thank God it's you! Oh Ed," and she sobbed into his shoulder as though her heart would break.

"It's OK my love. I've got you. I won't leave you. I'll never leave you again." He kissed the top of her head, murmuring sweet nothings into her hair and letting the tears fall freely down his own face.

The officers backed off as the two of them sat together in the wet sand, united at last in their grief. Ed held her tight and knew that nothing would ever come between them; he simply wouldn't allow it. He opened his eyes and looked down on her. She would need all his love and understanding over the weeks and months to come, and he promised himself that she would get it. A wave crept up the beach and washed around them. Something small pushed against Ed in the foam. He put his hand down and picked up Daz's wallet. No-one saw him. He quickly slipped it into his pocket and went back to comforting his girl.

The End